Dear Reader,

I love magic. It doesn't have to be the huge spells-and-flying-cats type of magic (although that all sounds great). But those moments of synchronicity, the mornings when you just know something good is going to happen, the nights when you and your oldest friend text at the same moment and then talk until dawn. And one of my favorite kinds of magic is the magic of the holidays.

In *The Lights on Knockbridge Lane*, that holiday magic brings single father Adam Mills and reclusive scientist Wes Mobray together. It gives Adam's daughter, Gus, a new family. And it teaches the residents of Knockbridge Lane that not every shy recluse who only comes out at night is a vampire. (I mean, I'm sure some of them are, but not Wes. :D)

For me, the magic of the holidays is that each one of us has a chance to see the world through the eyes of wonder, hope, and possibility—and what a better world it would be if we could do so all the time. So, brew some cocoa, curl up in front of the fire, and fall in love with magic right alongside Adam and Wes.

Welcome back to Garnet Run, Wyoming. I hope you'll stay awhile!

Cozy reading,

<3 *Roan*

RoanParrish.com

The Lights on Knockbridge Lane

ROAN PARRISH

HARLEQUIN
SPECIAL
EDITION

For my wonderful, supportive parents.

Recycling programs
for this product may
not exist in your area.

ISBN-13: 978-1-335-40812-9

The Lights on Knockbridge Lane

Copyright © 2021 by Roan Parrish

This edition published by arrangement with Harlequin Books S.A.

For questions and comments about the quality of this book,
please contact us at CustomerService@Harlequin.com.

Harlequin Enterprises ULC
22 Adelaide St. West, 40th Floor
Toronto, Ontario M5H 4E3, Canada
www.Harlequin.com

Printed in U.S.A.

Roan Parrish lives in Philadelphia, where she's gradually attempting to write love stories in every genre. When not writing, she can be found cutting her friends' hair, meandering through the city while listening to torch songs and melodic death metal, or cooking overly elaborate meals. She loves bonfires, winter beaches, minor chord harmonies, and self-tattooing. One time she may or may not have baked a six-layer chocolate cake and then thrown it out the window in a fit of pique.

Books by Roan Parrish

Harlequin Special Edition

The Lights on Knockbridge Lane

Carina Press

The Garnet Run series

Best Laid Plans
Better Than People

The Middle of Somewhere series

In the Middle of Somewhere
Out of Nowhere
Where We Left Off

Standalones

The Remaking of Corbin Wale
Natural Enemies
Heart of the Steal
Thrall

Visit the Author Profile page at Harlequin.com for more titles.

Garnet Run

1 Jack & Simon's house
2 Charlie & Rye's house
3 Dirt Road Cat Shelter
4 Cameron's house
5 Adam & Gus' house
6 Wes' house
7 Bram's house
8 Zachary's house

9 Grandma Jean's house
10 Van & Rachel's house
A Matheson's Hardware
B The Odeon Theater
C Miss Miriam's
D Sue's Bakery
E Pop's Pizza

F Crystal Bean Coffee Shop
G Garnet Run Public Library
H Smith's Market
I GR High
J Weird Antique Store
K GR Elementary
L Peach's Diner
M Bioluminescent clearing

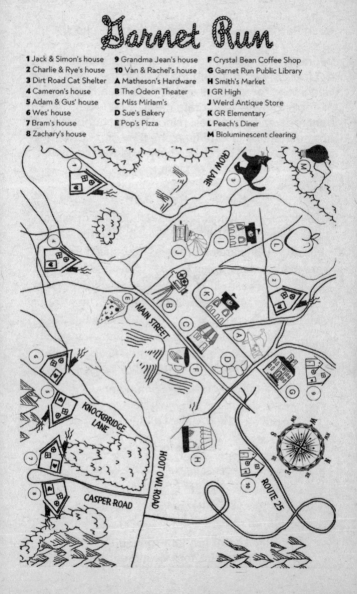

Chapter One

Adam

Everyone on Knockbridge Lane had a different theory about Westley Mobray. It was the first thing Adam Mills heard about as he introduced himself around last week, when he and August moved in.

The eight-year-old McKinnon twins next door said he was a vampire. Their parents, Darren and Rose McKinnon, scoffed at that, but said he could be a witch. Marisol Gutierrez three doors down insisted she'd seen him skulking around the neighborhood at night, hunting for animals to sacrifice to the devil. A teenager at the end of the street reported that anyone who looked him in the eyes would be hypnotized, and anyone who touched him would turn to stone. Mr. Montgomery on the corner just said *freak*.

Westley Mobray was never seen before sunset, though mysterious packages arrived on his doorstep often. He never spoke to anyone and never waved hello. And late at night, the windows of his run-down house glowed an eerie green.

At least, that's what they told Adam.

So when he saw the man in question through the

twilit haze of his own front window—with his daughter in tow—he was understandably startled. Especially since he'd thought she was playing quietly in her room.

He'd slammed two coffees to prevent it, but he'd been asleep. The kind of light, unsatisfying sleep he often fell into when he had a moment of quiet. Which was something that didn't happen that often as the newly single parent of an eight-year-old.

His insomnia had been pretty bad since the divorce, and worse since they moved back to Garnet Run, where he was the only one responsible for Gus.

The knock at the door jerked him out of that strange sleep, and he scrambled for the door, stubbing his toe in the process, so that when he yanked it open he was biting back the kind of words that he tried with varying degrees of success not to say in front of Gus.

He focused on Gus first. She was all in one piece and was even smiling. It was her *I did something bad and delightful* smile, but a smile was good—at least when on a child who seemed to have been forcibly dragged home by an irate stranger.

"Where is your coat?" is what came out of Adam's mouth.

Sometimes he tried to remember what it was like when he talked about things like the composition of his next shot, which restaurant's tiramisu he preferred, or the latest cozy mystery he was reading.

Now he said things like "Where is your coat" and "Don't take that apart" and "If you don't stop making that sound I might have to throttle you." Okay, he didn't say the last one so much as think it. Often.

"It's not that cold," his wonderful, brilliant daughter said, her lips only vaguely blue.

Adam counseled himself to breathe.

Once he'd determined that Gus was all in one piece and frostbite wasn't imminent, he turned his attention to the man who'd brought her home.

"Um," he said intelligently.

Westley Mobray was tall and severe, with shaved dark hair and strong dark eyebrows over piercing blue eyes. Those eyes were narrowed slightly, either in anger or—if the neighborhood rumors were to be believed—because he never went outside when there was the slightest bit of light still in the sky, as it would, of course, burn him to ash.

"She broke into my house," he said. His voice was low and rough with disuse.

"She's eight."

Mobray cocked his head as if unsure what that might have to do with Gus' felonious misdeeds.

Adam sighed.

"Gus, did you break into our neighbor's house?"

She squinted and screwed up her face in a way that said she absolutely had. Adam and Gus had a strict No Lying policy, which had resulted in Gus developing a keen sense of words and their exact meanings.

"I didn't break anything," she settled on finally.

Adam offered up a silent prayer to the universe that his daughter not end up in prison.

"Did you enter without being invited?" he clarified.

And the vampire hits just kept coming.

She bit her lip and nodded.

"You can't do that, baby. It's not safe for you and it's not okay to intrude on other people's privacy."

She looked down at her toes, the very image of contrition. Then she peeked up at him with a glint in her big blue eyes.

"But he has lizards," she said softly.

"Okay, let's get you inside," Adam said quickly. Once Gus got going on something that fascinated her—and lizards were the most recent addition to that list—she tended to forget any reason why she shouldn't abandon all sense (or rules) to pursue it.

Adam passed her behind him and looked up at Westley Mobray.

"I'm really sorry about that," he said.

"She climbed in through my basement window."

Adam winced. Gus really was remarkably resourceful. And limber.

"I'm so sorry. I'll talk to her. She just, uh, *really* likes lizards. It started as a dinosaur thing and now... Anyway. Eight-year-olds."

The mysterious neighbor didn't say anything, just continued to look at Adam with a keen, curious gaze.

"I don't think I'm hypnotized," Adam muttered. Would you know if you were hypnotized, or was that part of hypnosis?

"Excuse me?" Westley Mobray said.

"Uh, nothing. Thanks for bringing her home. I'm Adam Mills, by the way." He stuck out his hand.

"We just moved here. That's Gus. August. But she likes Gus."

Mobray didn't shake Adam's hand—so Adam wouldn't feel his preternatural chill?—so he shoved it in his pocket. But at least there was no chance he'd turn to stone.

"Wes," said the man who was probably not a vampire or a witch or a Medusa. Freak? Well, the jury was out. But Adam tended to like freaks.

Then he turned and walked away, broad shoulders blocking the last of the day's light.

Inside, Gus had helped herself to a glass of apple juice and she held up the bottle to Adam angelically, to ask if he wanted some.

He nodded and she poured him some juice. He rummaged around in the disordered cabinets, looking for something to fix for dinner.

"Gus," he began, assuming the lecture would flow naturally once he opened his mouth.

"Daddy, he has the *best* basement," Gus gushed. "*Four* lizards. One has orange and black on its back and one is red and the other two are brown and he has a *snake*—I don't know what kind—and he showed me a huge, hairy spider!"

Adam choked on his juice.

He did not, historically, care for spiders.

"A, um, spider?" he squeaked.

"A turanyulla," she confirmed.

"Tarantula," he corrected automatically. "You saw this when you climbed in the window?"

"He showed me the tarantula." She said the word slowly and carefully. "He put it right in my face!"

Said face was lit with joy. Adam's stomach dropped. "He *what*?"

"I'm sorry I climbed in. It was just *so interesting*."

Interesting was Gus' buzzword. She had discovered, rightfully, that Adam liked when she was interested in things. Now she used it like a shovel to dig herself out of every mess she got in.

"So the, er, tarantula was placed near your, um, face?" His voice broke at the end.

"He thought it would scare me." She grinned hugely. "But it was *so* cool."

"Come," he wheezed. He grabbed her hand, burst through the door and stalked to the last house on the street. Damn, it *was* cold.

Wes Mobray's house certainly did nothing to discourage rumors of his supernatural being. It was a two-story Craftsman cottage, like the one he and Gus were renting. But unlike theirs, which was painted in cheery white and blue, it wore a peeling coat of brown, and every window but two—one that must have been Gus' basement ingress, and one small upstairs window—was covered from the inside with brown paper.

The whole thing gave the house the look of a crumpled paper bag. A crumpled gothic paper bag.

Adam felt a momentary pang of pity for Wes Mobray. Maligned and gossiped about by neighbors, living in this depressing paper bag of a house… But then he remembered what had brought him over here and he steeled himself to ring the doorbell.

It took ages, but after several more rings and some angry knocking, the door creaked open and Wes Mobray peered out, looking very confused.

"You!" Adam accused with a practiced pointer finger to Wes' face. "Put a *tarantula* in my daughter's *face*?!"

"She broke into my house," he said simply.

"I don't care. You do *not* shove *poisonous*, *terrifying*—" Adam shuddered "—*creepy* spiders in children's faces!"

"You're scared of spiders."

The man's infuriatingly handsome face quirked with the hint of a smile. Adam felt parts of himself turn just the tiniest bit to stone. He squared his shoulders and drew himself up to his full (admittedly not terribly imposing) height.

He looked Westley Mobray dead in his rather beautiful eyes and said firmly and with utter conviction: "Yes. I am terrified of them."

Chapter Two

Adam

Adam's younger sibling, River, was a literal angel.

"You," Adam told them, "are a literal angel."

They rolled their eyes but looked pleased.

Adam had grown up in Garnet Run, but left for Boulder, Colorado as soon as he turned eighteen. He left partly to escape his parents and partly because Garnet Run felt small and isolated and conservative, and yeah, okay, partly because he met the new boy in town and followed him, thinking they'd be together forever, like in the swoony old Hollywood romances that his grandmother favored.

And they were together, for a while.

But when he and Mason divorced, there was no way Adam could stay in Boulder. No way he could take care of Gus by himself on a freelance photographer's salary, and no way he could work a full-time job without childcare, which, of course, he couldn't afford.

River was the main reason he'd decided to move back. They loved Gus and when Adam called them to tell them it was over with Mason, the first thing they said—even before *Sorry*—was *I'm here to help.*

It had made Adam cry then and it still made him a little misty now. River was only twenty, but already a lifesaver. It helped that Gus adored them right back.

River had gotten Adam a job at a local hardware store through their friend Rye. And every day, they picked Gus up from school and stayed with her for an hour until Adam got home from work.

He'd tried to pay them the first three days and they'd turned him down flat. Yesterday, they'd told him to stop offering. Today, before he could open his mouth, they clapped their hand over it, and said, "Shh."

Seriously: angel.

"How's the kitten biz?" Adam asked.

River's eyes lit up. They worked as the manager of The Dirt Road Cat Shelter. River'd always loved animals so it was a dream job.

Before Adam knew it, they'd pushed their phone into his hand and were scrolling through pictures and videos of utterly adorable kittens and cats, introducing them to him and describing their antics.

"I should bring Gus by someday to see all the kitties," he mused.

"You can," River said. "But I don't think she's that interested in cats."

The child in question came into the kitchen then, wearing her hangry face, and Adam jumped up to start dinner.

"You staying?" he asked River.

They shook their head and kissed him on the cheek. "Gotta run."

"Thank you!" Adam called after them, putting water on to boil.

Gus pouted and slumped against the counter dramatically.

"What's up, baby?"

"Nothing," she sighed.

"How's school?"

"Stupid."

"You know I don't like that word," he told her gently. "Can you be more specific?"

"I already did this science lesson at home," she said dejectedly.

Adam winced. *Home* meant back in Boulder.

"And everyone is boring."

He wanted so badly to tell her it wasn't true. That there were kids here who could be her best friends if she'd let them.

But he remembered too well being the odd one out in elementary school. (Not to mention middle school and high school.) He remembered how lonely it felt when other kids weren't interested in the same things. When they thought you were weird.

"Maybe if you talk to them about things you're interested in, you'll make them interested too," he offered.

Gus thought about that.

"Maybe," she reluctantly allowed. After a minute, her eyes lit with excitement in a way that warmed Adam's heart—and then made him suspicious. "Be back," she murmured, and ran to her room.

* * *

"I need to put this in Mr. Wes' mailbox," Gus informed Adam the next morning as they left for school.

She held up a construction paper packet sealed with so many stickers they were overlapping like tape. It said *IMPORTANT* on it in all caps red marker.

Adam opened the mailbox so she could shove the sticky package inside, wondering if he should've asked to know what it was first. But since he was certain it wasn't a bomb or anything dangerous—okay, like, ninety-nine percent certain—he let Gus have her privacy.

Well, ninety-five percent.

"What was that, baby?" he asked casually.

"Secret," she said.

"It isn't, um, anything he won't like, is it?" *Or anything on the FBI watch list?*

"No," she said with certainty. "He will definitely like it."

Gus was sulking when Adam got home from work.

"What happened?" he asked River.

They shrugged. "She looked in the mailbox like five times but wouldn't say what she was looking for."

At dinner, Gus picked at her food.

"He didn't write back," she said finally, looking dejected.

"Wes?"

She nodded and Adam's heart broke. He wanted to strangle their neighbor. He wanted to punch the hell out of him for causing his kid one second of pain. Obviously, he would do neither, since it was totally reasonable not to immediately respond to a strange kid within twelve hours of receiving a mysterious marker-scrawled missive.

"Maybe he didn't check his mail yet," he offered. "Not everyone checks quite as often as you do." *Especially if they only go out at night and are busy hunting for animals to sacrifice to the devil.* Adam amused himself.

Gus cheered up.

"Oh, yeah!" she said. "Probably we should ring his doorbell and give it to him in person."

"Listen, kiddo. I know you want to see those lizards and the—" He swallowed hard. "Tarantula again. But Wes is a stranger. He seems like he enjoys being left alone. You know how sometimes you want to be alone in your room?"

She rolled her eyes and nodded.

"Wes feels that way about his house. So it's okay to put a letter in the mailbox. But we can't bother him at home."

She sighed the sigh of injustice, but nodded again.

After a few unenthusiastic bites of macaroni, she said, "Papa doesn't want to be bothered either."

And Adam's heart broke all over again. Because Wes Mobray might not have had any responsibility toward Gus. But Mason? Mason absolutely did.

Mason had said he would call the night they arrived in Garnet Run, and hadn't. Gus had called him instead. Mason had said she could call him anytime she wanted. When she FaceTimed, he usually didn't pick up the phone.

"Papa loves you, Gus. But he's not the best at doing everything he says he will. It's not you."

A tear ran down her cheek to salt the macaroni.

"He got rid of us."

She said it so fiercely and with such certainty that it startled Adam. And it was true, in its way. From the moment he got River's call about their sister, Marina, Adam had burned with purpose. Marina couldn't take care of Gus, but he could. He *wanted* to. And he'd assumed that Mason would want to as well. It had been a mistake—a genuine one, but a mistake nonetheless, and as much as he wished he could blame Mason for that, it was undeniably reasonable for a young man who'd never thought about kids to be less than enthusiastic about suddenly having one.

No, it wasn't Mason's ambivalence that Adam resented. It was that for a few years, he'd seemed committed. After his initial shock, he'd simply said, "We'll make it work." And for a little while, it had.

Mason's uneven attention and affection had been enough—just enough, but enough—for Gus to want more. Just enough to honor the letter of the agreement he and Adam had struck. For every dinner he ate out and play time he worked through, Mason was there with a few minutes of attention so intense that it seemed like it had lasted far longer; a gift that came at just the right moment.

It would have been better, Adam thought, if Mason had said from the beginning that he had no interest in this life. Better if Gus had never had to experi-ence the singular cruelty of parental rejection. His blood boiled.

He grabbed Gus and pulled her into his arms.

He started to tell her no. To tell her it wasn't like that.

But Gus put her small, slightly sticky hands on his cheeks and looked directly into his eyes.

"No lying," she said, voice flinty and far too adult. "Not ever."

"Okay, no lying."

Adam squared his shoulders and looked right back into her eyes. His sister Marina's eyes. There was no point in explaining that, yes, Mason had gotten rid of them, bit by bit, over the years, but that it had been Adam, finally, who gave the ultimatum: I choose Gus over you, so either choose Gus over all the rest of it, or we're gone. No need to give Gus one more reason to feel like this was because of her. Besides, it was just as likely she would end up angry at him for tak-ing her papa away.

So he told the only truth he was absolutely sure of.

"We're going to have the best time just the two of us. It's going to be Christmas soon, and we're going to have so much fun. I love you to the moon and back, and nothing will ever change that."

There was a flicker in her eyes at *Christmas*.

"What kind of fun?" she asked, not yet convinced.

Unprepared for the question, Adam said vaguely, "Oh, all kinds."

"Can you be more specific?" she demanded, echoing his own words back to him, curse her.

"What would be the most fun for you? If you could do one special thing."

Gus thought hard. She put her elbows on the table and her chin in her hands. And then she looked at Adam, eyes glistening with her earlier emotion, and made a somber declaration.

"I want our house to have the most Christmas lights of any house in the world."

Adam swallowed hard. *It could have been so much worse!* he told himself. She could have wished to turn her bedroom into an entomology laboratory or learn to ride a motorcycle. This was fine.

Adam's mission was clear: in order to convince his daughter that they could still have a wonderful Christmas despite leaving Mason, their home, and all their friends far behind them, he just had to find a way to procure the most Christmas lights in the whole world.

What could possibly go wrong?

Chapter Three

Wes

As the sun set outside his house on Knockbridge Lane, Wes Mobray came alive.

He'd always preferred going out at night. Not because—as his neighbors believed—he was a vampire or a witch or whatever the rumor of the moment was. But because nighttime was peaceful, quiet, and blissfully free of human interaction.

No doorbells ringing or neighbors shouting; no telemarketers or music blasting; no smiling, chatting, questioning, *people*. No one looking at him.

Just peaceful, calm darkness in which to wander in the woods, collect dirt samples, or source small rodents.

Wes' doorbell rang.

He froze.

It couldn't be James with the compost; he knew better than to ring the bell. There must be a new delivery person on his route; all the regulars knew to simply leave his packages outside the front door. But winter was tricky: it got dark early enough that people thought it was still okay to intrude. When whoever it was realized he wasn't going to answer, surely they'd go away.

Wes turned his attention to chopping his food waste from the previous day to add to the biogas generator.

The doorbell rang again.

Wes stalked to the front door and threw it open, ready to inform the new FedEx employee of the agreement he had that his packages simply be left outside without disturbing him.

But it wasn't a delivery person. It was the new kid from across the street who'd crawled through his basement window.

She stood on his front stoop, arms crossed and face twisted in a scowl.

"You didn't write me back," she said, and her voice was softer than her posture, like perhaps anger was a cover for disappointment. Sadness. Wes was familiar.

"What?"

"Didn't you get my letter?"

Wes glanced at the mailbox he never checked. Anything he cared about came through via email.

"No."

"Oh. That's what Daddy said."

As if conjured by his title, the father in question came running across the street.

Wes had watched Adam Mills move in the week before through the periscope mounted on the side of his house. He might not have wanted anyone to look at him, but he certainly watched them.

Adam and his daughter had arrived in a medium

moving van, and Adam had unloaded his belongings himself, with the help of one other person. He had introduced himself to every single neighbor that happened past.

Only of course they hadn't *happened* past—they had coordinated trips to the mailbox and the grocery store with times when Adam was outside, so they could scope out the new addition to Knockbridge Lane.

Wes had lived here for four years. He knew the routine. They'd tried it on him too. And they'd failed. But Adam was friendly. Talkative.

Normal.

"Gus, Jesus, you scared the sh— You scared me," he said.

Adam Mills jogged up the steps and glared at his daughter.

"What did I tell you?" he demanded.

"I know, Daddy, but I just *had* to," Gus said.

Father and daughter seemed to be having an intense conversation made of looks and facial expressions.

Wes cleared his throat.

"I'm really sorry," Adam told him, and slid a hand around Gus' small shoulder.

"It's in your mailbox," Gus said. "Write me back, okay?"

She looked so intent that for a moment Wes considered that perhaps this was a cry for help. But then she pouted at him and spoke sweetly.

"Couldn't we *please* see your taranula again? Just for a second?"

"Tarantula," Wes corrected. He shot a glance at Adam, who had gone pale and shrunk backward, hand that had been on Gus' shoulder hanging in the empty air.

"No, no," Adam said desperately. "We can't bother Mr. Mobray."

Gus put her hands together and bounced in place, mouthing *please* over and over.

Wes was just about to close the door in her wide-eyed little face. Then, inside the house, something exploded.

Wes bolted inside and ran to the room that housed the biogas generator.

He'd had a problem with a leaky valve between the slurry and gas storage before, but that shouldn't have been explosive.

As he rounded the corner, the scene before him came into focus: one splodge of wet compost goo on the floor and a splatter on the wall, one tube that should have been connected flapping free, and one hognose snake hanging from the chandelier, hissing at the raccoon below.

"Oh, dear god—" came Adam's voice behind him, while at the same time Gus said, "A snake! Can I touch it!?"

Wes wheeled around and glared at them. Who just waltzed into other people's houses?

"Sorry!" Adam said, putting his hands up. "We wanted to make sure you didn't blow up."

"I wanted to see the tarantula," Gus confessed.

Wes found himself in an octagon of things out of place. Agitated and flustered as he was, though, he couldn't resist the clarion call of a kid who was fascinated by snakes and spiders like he had always been.

"Her name's Bettie," Wes said grudgingly. "She's sleeping right now."

"Who's that?" Gus pointed.

"Milford," Wes said shortly. But her interest didn't waver, so he grudgingly elaborated. "She's a *Heterodon platirhinos*—a hognose snake, about thirty-six inches long."

"Is that perhaps a...raccoon?" Adam asked. While Gus had come closer with each word, Adam had retreated to the farthest corner of the room and fitted himself into it.

"Janice."

"Oh, sure," Adam murmured weakly. "She's tame, then?"

Wes shrugged. Humans' estimation of tameness was variable and useless.

"Is that what exploded?" Gus asked, gazing raptly at the biogas generator.

Wes nodded.

Gus screwed up her face. "What is it?"

"It's a biogas generator," Wes said. When she crept closer to it, Wes found himself helpless in the face of her curiosity. "It converts food and herbaceous waste into methane that I can use for power."

Gus blinked, cocked her head, and said politely, "Can you use other words?"

"She's eight," Adam said.

Gus was looking up at him, all big-eyed attention, and Wes realized she actually was interested.

"As things decompose—rot—like in the trash, gasses form. One of those gasses is methane. I keep my rotting, uh, stuff, in this container and when the gas is produced, it inflates this rubber thing here, and creates pressure. That pressure can bring that gas to the stove or a light—whatever I want."

"From trash?" Gus said in wonder.

"Yeah. It's basically like a giant stomach. Just like food breaks down in your stomach and creates gas, which expands your stomach, and the pressure makes you…um."

He wasn't sure what the proper word was for a kid.

She giggled. "Fart?! That's why people fart?" She whirled around. "Daddy, that's why people fart!?"

"I…to be honest, I didn't know that, sweetie." Adam looked to Wes. "Do you run your stove off this generator?"

"No, not the stove. That was just an example. I could. But this is an experiment."

"Experiment in what?" Adam asked as Gus, apparently having lost interest in the biogas generator, said, "Can I hold that spider now, please?"

"Oops, we gotta go now," Adam said instantly.

"Daddy's very scared of spiders," Gus whispered completely audibly. "But can I?"

Bettie was a sweet, shy creature who liked to crawl slowly around the perimeter of the house as if she were keeping watch. She didn't like sudden movement or loud noises, and a child seemed a guarantor of both. Wes didn't want to let Gus hold her.

But most children—most people—thought of tarantulas as terrifying, dangerous threats. The fact that Gus was interested in her rather than scared made him happy.

"If I let you hold her, you have to be very, very still," Wes said seriously. "It tickles when she crawls, but you can't jerk your hand back or scream or throw her."

His heart began to pound at the idea of his sweet baby being squished or thrown by a careless hand.

"Maybe it's not a good idea," he said, reconsidering.

"I won't," Gus said solemnly. "I promise."

Wes took a moment to plan precisely how he would swoop in and rescue Bettie at the first sign of trouble.

"Gosh, um," Adam said weakly from the corner. "I'll just…"

He began to edge toward the front door, shoulder blades glued to the wall. That was the typical response.

Wes went into the kitchen where he'd last seen Bettie. She was on the windowsill, looking regal in repose.

"Hi, baby," he said softly, running a finger down her back. "You okay?"

Bettie crawled onto his hand, her body a velvet weight in his palm.

In the other room, Adam was almost to the front door. Even though Wes thought tarantulas were amazing and beautiful creatures, he did understand the fear of them was significant, and he didn't want to upset Adam. He seemed like a sweet man. A caring, kind man. Even if he had pushed his way into Wes' house.

So instead of holding his hand palm-up so Adam couldn't help but see Bettie crawl, Wes angled his body between Adam and his lightly cupped hand.

"Oh, god," Adam wheezed. "I'm so sorry, I just… *ugh*."

"Oh, Daddy," Gus said absently. Then, "Ooh, she's so cool."

The sound of a slamming door echoed through the house.

"Put your hand down on the table," Wes said.

Gus put her hand down, palm-up, and Wes deposited Bettie a few inches away.

Bettie crept close, then felt Gus' finger with her front legs. Gus' eyes got wide.

"How old is she?"

"I'm not exactly sure. I've had her for about ten years. Females can live to be thirty or so, though."

"Why's her name Bettie?"

"Why is your name Gus?"

"It's short for August."

"It's short for Elizabeth," he retorted, which wasn't true.

"But *why*?"

Wes stared and Gus stared right back. But she still didn't move her hand, which Bettie was crawling onto.

Wes scrubbed a hand over his shorn hair. He didn't

care to untangle the serpentine path his brain had taken to associate the tarantula with Bettie Page, especially since an eight-year-old would surely have no idea who she was.

"She just," he said slowly. "She looked like a Bettie."

Gus nodded, accepting that answer.

For a while she observed Bettie closely, not seeming to see anything else.

"My mom named me August," she said finally, stroking Bettie with a gentle finger. "Cuz I was born in August."

"Your mom doesn't live with you guys?" Wes heard himself ask.

He made it a habit not to initiate conversations, but the kid was already in his house, and he found himself oddly curious about Gus and Adam Mills.

Gus shook her head.

"I never lived with her. Daddy took me right after I was born. My mom is Daddy's sister, but we're not friends. She lives in Cheyenne, but I don't see her. I'm friends with River, though. River's Daddy's other sibling. Daddy says River's a literal angel. They watch me after school now that we don't live at home anymore."

Wes smiled at *literal angel*.

"Where's home?"

"Where we used to live in Colorado. With Daddy and Papa."

She frowned and got quiet.

Wes didn't know what made him ask the next question. As a rule, he didn't ask personal questions of strangers. People tended to take them as an invitation to ask questions of their own.

"Your dad's gay?"

Gus' eyes shot to his, her expression utterly fierce, though the hand holding Bettie remained completely still.

"Yeah. You gotta problem with that?"

If looks could maim, he'd've been on the floor right now. Wes admired her protectiveness.

"No. No."

In fact, his heart was beating faster for quite the opposite reason.

"You better not be mean to my daddy," Gus said, still vivisecting him with her stare.

And Wes found himself in the strange position of wishing he had someone as fierce as this tiny eight-year-old to have his back.

"I won't," Wes said. "I promise."

That seemed to placate Gus.

"Speaking of which, you should probably go make sure he's okay."

She sighed.

"Yeah. Poor Daddy. He was *so* scared."

She grinned at him conspiratorially. Wes was surprised to find himself smiling back at her.

"He really was."

Very slowly and carefully, Gus stood up and deposited Bettie in Wes' outstretched hand.

"Thanks for letting me hold her," Gus said, and headed for the front door.

With her hand on the knob, she turned back to look at him.

"Can I come back sometime? Hold her again?"

Wes saw the hope in her eyes and even though it went against every instinct of privacy and self-preservation he'd cultivated in the four years since leaving LA for Garnet Run, Wyoming, he said, "Yeah, okay."

Chapter Four

Adam

It was absolutely essential that Adam distract Gus from her burgeoning obsession with Wes Mobray, and, by extension, her obsession with—Adam gulped at the thought—tarantulas. And honoring her Christmas wish was just the way to do it.

"Hey, Charlie," Adam asked his new boss. "Do we have more Christmas lights?"

"More than the ones on display?" he asked patiently, gesturing to the charmingly lumberjack-esque holiday display at the front of the store. It was only the beginning of November, but people were already decorating.

Matheson's Hardware had been around for as long as Adam could remember, but he'd never set foot inside it until River got him an interview with owner Charlie Matheson last week.

Charlie was a big bear of a guy who was helpful and kind to every customer and then turned around and was equally helpful and kind to everyone else. It was pretty endearing. Especially when that extended to giving Adam a job even though what he knew about hardware could fit on the head of a nail. A penny nail. (See, he learned that lingo on his first day at work.)

Charlie's partner, Rye, had started The Dirt Road Cat Shelter, which River managed, and River spoke of him in reverent tones. It seemed it was Rye Adam was replacing, as he didn't have time to work at Matheson's anymore, given how well the shelter was doing.

Rye was heavily tattooed, with long, messy dark hair and eyes the uncanny gray of a morning storm. He tended to glare a lot, seemingly without ire, but he'd grinned wryly when he met Adam.

"It's perfect," Rye had told him. "I didn't know shit about the hardware biz. Now that I'm leaving, of course Charlie should hire someone else who doesn't know shit."

Whatever Charlie's reasons—and Adam was pretty sure it was wanting to help out River as much as to give a job to another queer person—Adam was supremely grateful and was doing his level best never to give Charlie reason to regret it.

The holiday display did indeed feature Christmas lights, as well as a beautiful wooden cutout of a log cabin, painted in full color, on which a string of lights was draped. Whenever anyone commented on it, Charlie proudly informed them that his brother, Jack, had painted it.

"Yeah, I guess I was wondering if there might be a way to get them cheaper if I order some directly from the distributor. If that's not overstepping," Adam added. He *had* only been working there for a week.

"I'm really sorry, Adam." Charlie looked genuinely disappointed. "I pretty much sell these at cost. Around the holidays they're a sure sell, so I use them to get people in the door, but I don't mark them up."

"Oh. That's okay. I'll just buy some of these, then."

He bought ten boxes of lights with his employee discount. There went the day's pay, but he couldn't wait to see the smile on Gus' face when he brought them home.

The scent of snow was in the air when Adam pulled up to his house. Inside, lights glowed warmly, but he found himself glancing across the street at Wes' house, which stood dark and still.

For all that he wanted Gus to forget the lure of Wes' unusual critters, Adam couldn't forget the way Wes had cradled his pet so gently in his large hand. The way he'd explained his…whatever that thing had been to Gus patiently and as if she could understand everything he was saying.

Mason had not been patient. Not with Gus and definitely not with Adam.

"Hey," Adam called as he unlocked the door. "Where's my little monster?"

A giggle, then the rush of footsteps, and Adam turned around to see not Gus, but River, with their arms outflung like a child.

Adam grinned and Gus peeked from around the corner, hand over her mouth to muffle her laughter.

"There you are!" Adam cried, playing along. "Come here, my little monster."

He threw his arms around River and hugged them tight. River tensed for a moment and Adam started to let go, but then they relaxed into his arms. Adam squeezed his younger sibling tight for a few more seconds, then let them go with a ruffle of their hair. He hadn't had the chance to do that much in their lives spent mostly apart, and spared a moment of gratitude that he now had the chance.

"No, me!" Gus yelled, running straight at Adam and plastering herself to him.

"Here's my other little monster."

She nodded and he swung her around until they were both dizzy.

"What's that?" Gus asked, recovering quickly, pointing at the large brown paper bag with Matheson's Hardware stamped on it.

"Look inside."

She poked her nose inside and grinned.

"Lights for me!"

"Lights for us," Adam said.

"Lights for us," Gus echoed politely. Then, to River she said, "I'm gonna make our house have the most Christmas lights in history."

"Whoa," River said. "That sounds beautiful!" They turned to Adam and added under their breath, "And expensive."

Adam grimaced. He hadn't quite realized the expense when he'd agreed to this project.

"Can we put them up?"

Gus was already tearing open the boxes.

"Sure. You wanna help?" Adam asked River.

"Nah, I'm gonna take off. Gotta check on Hydra."

"I hope that's a cat?"

River flushed. "Yeah. Bye."

"Bye, River!" Gus yelled without looking up from her task.

Lights freed from their boxes, they went outside. Immediately, Adam realized their first problem: he didn't have a ladder.

"Shoot, sorry, sweetheart. I'll get one from work tomorrow."

Adam quickly budgeted for that and wondered if Charlie would lend him one, just for the weekend.

"Maybe Wes has one," Gus suggested slyly.

"Er, maybe one of our other neighbors—"

"I'll ask!"

And with that she ran off. Gus knew he should stop her, but he couldn't deny that mysterious, reclusive, frankly weird Wes Mobray had gotten under his skin.

Instead, Adam followed his daughter to Wes' front door. It opened faster this time, and Wes looked less confused to find them there.

"Hi," he said, his frown only at twenty-five percent this time.

One of the neighbors Adam hadn't met yet—a woman who lived with her daughter at the end of Knockbridge Lane—drove past and craned her neck to look at them.

Adam raised a hand in greeting, and she snapped her eyes front. Wes took a step back into the shadows of the house.

"We're hanging Christmas lights," Gus announced. "Wanna help?"

"Oh, honey, that's not— We don't— I thought— Um, we were wondering if you had a ladder we could borrow. You don't have to— That is, you can if you want, but—"

Adam physically forced his lips together to prevent more gibberish from leaking out. Wes was looking at him intently. Then he glanced at Gus. She was vibrating in place like a whippet in a snowstorm, eyes huge and hopeful.

"Um. Okay," Wes said.

Adam gaped.

"Yay! Yes! Yay!" Gus cried, and darted inside. "Can I see Bettie?"

Adam and Wes looked at each other and Adam felt like Wes could see right through him.

"You don't have to," Adam said. "I just. I accidentally promised Gus the biggest Christmas light display in the world and, uh."

Every time he said it out loud it sounded more unrealistic than the last.

Wes raised an eyebrow but said nothing. He kept looking at Adam like there was a mystery he was trying to solve.

"Wes!" Gus' voice sounded more distant. "Can I touch this snake?!"

"Oh god, I'm sorry," Adam said. Then the words registered, and panic ripped through him. "Wait, snake?"

"She's not poisonous, don't worry."

That was actually *not* what Adam's reaction had been in response to, but he made himself nod calmly.

"Good, good."

"Are you coming in, or?"

"Oh, nah, I'll just wait here," Adam said extremely casually. "Don't mind me. Yep. Fresh air. I'll just. Uh-huh, here's great."

Wes smiled for the first time and it was like nothing Adam had ever seen.

His face lit with tender humor, eyes crinkling at the corners and full lips parting to reveal charmingly crooked teeth. *Damn*, he was beautiful.

"Wes, Wes!" Gus ran up behind him and skidded to a halt inches before she would've slammed into him. "Can I?"

"You can touch her while I get the ladder," Wes said.

Gus turned to Adam.

"Daddy, do you wanna touch the snake? She's *so* cool."

Adam's skin crawled.

"Nope, you go ahead."

Adam sank down to sit at the top step and wait. The sun was setting, and it painted the expanse of Knockbridge Lane in muted pinks and purples. The mountains rose to the west, and to the north and east were trees. A Cooper's hawk glided in a wide arc high above the tallest branches.

It was beautiful here, there was no denying. Adam hadn't left all those years ago because it wasn't a beautiful place to live. But no amount of natural beauty could make up for living with parents like his.

The door opened and Gus barreled out.

"Oh my god, Daddy. She sat around my neck like a scarf!"

Gus' eyes were bright as stars, so Adam swallowed down his nausea and smiled right back.

"That's so cool!" he said weakly.

"So. Cool." Gus shivered with delight. "You know how everyone said Wes was a vampire and a witch and stuff?"

"You know better than to believe everything people say, don't you?" Adam admonished.

"I know." Gus waved him away. "I was gonna say, I think he's more like a superhero. He has all these sidekicks, and he knows how to do *everything*."

Gus pulled the door shut and skipped toward the garage. Adam trailed along in her wake. He was embarrassed to admit it, but he was just the tiniest bit jealous of his daughter's worship of Wes.

Wes came out carrying a ladder, a hammer, and some nails.

"Penny nails," Adam said absently.

When they'd lugged the ladder across the street and stood in front of their house, Adam said, "Okay, Gus, your call. Where are they going?"

"Can I go on the ladder?" she asked excitedly, eyes wide.

"Er, no, baby. Sorry, it's too dangerous." She pouted but shrugged. "Because I might have a heart attack," he muttered.

"Let me guess," Wes said. "You don't like heights?"

Adam rounded on him, instantly defensive.

"Why would you say that?"

His whole life people had looked at his small stature and his sexual orientation and his sensitivity and assumed he was weak and scared.

And yeah, okay, he *was* afraid of some things. But it was natural to be afraid. There was nothing wrong with it. Tarantulas and snakes could be *poisonous*. It was self-preservation to fear them. He wasn't upset that he was afraid of things; he was upset that people thought being afraid meant being weak.

And Adam Mills was definitely not weak.

Wes looked taken aback. "You just seemed really worried about Gus going up, so I thought… I don't know. Sorry."

Adam internally cringed at himself for being so defensive.

"Oh. Right. Um, no problem. That's just because she's, you know, a very small child."

Wes nodded.

"I don't really know much about children."

"Surely you at least were one?" Adam said, trying to lighten the mood he'd cast in darkness.

Wes just blinked. "Not this kind."

"What kind?"

He shrugged, and walked onto the porch, then around the side of the house.

"Here's your outlet," he said.

Gus pointed to the front of the house. "Let's put them there, like an outline of light."

Adam nodded and gathered the lights under his arm. Then he began to ascend the ladder.

The truth? Was that Adam *was* afraid of heights. But he would be goddamned if he was going to admit that in front of Wes now.

"Are you okay, Daddy?"

Gus sounded concerned and Adam realized he'd stopped four rungs up the ladder.

"Uh-huh, fine." His voice broke but he made himself keep climbing.

From the top of the ladder, Adam surveyed the neighborhood below him.

This, it turned out, was a huge mistake.

"Oh god, oh god, ohgod, ohgodohgod. It's tall. This is tall. High. Up here. This is *dangerous*! How many people die each year in routine Christmas decorating accidents?!"

"Careful, Daddy," Gus said.

Wes said, "Three hundred ladder-related fatalities annually in the US. Hmm, I would've thought it'd be higher."

Adam squeezed his eyes shut and forced himself to unclench the claw of his fist from around the lights enough to find the end of the strand.

"Here's ten years of Christmas-related injuries." Wes scrolled on his phone. "Wow, 134,281 people were sent to the ER with holiday decoration–related injuries from 2008 to 2017. God, who knew."

Adam's whole body was rigid, and he heard himself make a tiny whimpering sound that he hoped didn't reach the ground.

"They're not straight, Daddy," Gus called helpfully from the ground.

Adam, who was at the moment trying to figure out how on earth it was humanly possible to lift a string of lights, unpocket a nail, hammer in said nail, string the lights on the nail, and move the ladder to another position without falling to his death, just said, "Thank you, baby."

After a great deal of ladder moving (because no, thank you, Wes, Adam did not want to simply climb onto the roof), thumb hammering, and light adjusting, Adam got all ten strands of lights hung.

He climbed down the ladder slowly, feeling extremely pleased with himself. Triumphant, even!

He let out a pleased sigh, slung his arm around Gus' shoulders, and looked up at what he'd just accomplished.

And looked.

And tilted his head and looked some more.

"Huh," he said.

"Hmm," Wes echoed.

The ten strands of lights barely outlined the front triangle of the roof, and even though they twinkled merrily in the darkness, the lights looked sparse against the clear sky full of stars.

"That," Gus declared, "is *not* the most lights in the world."

Which, frankly, was what they were all thinking.

"We'll get more, sweetie," Adam said, wanting to cling to the sense of triumph he'd felt only seconds before. "This is just a start."

Gus nodded seriously.

"Okay," she said.

The *okay* got him. Gus trusted that if he said something would happen, it *would* happen. He treasured her trust more even than her love. It was something he would never betray.

Which just meant he needed to figure out a way to acquire more lights. Lots more. So many more that whenever Gus looked at them, she would stop thinking about Boulder and their house there. She would stop thinking about the friends she'd left behind. And most of all, she'd stop thinking about Mason, her papa who, when Adam's ultimatum came—be a part of their family or have no say in it—chose a life of freedom over being a father.

So many more that Gus would gaze at them and think only about how beautiful it was here, and how cozy their little house was. What a great holiday they would have together. And how very, very much Adam loved her.

Now if he could just figure out how to do that without bankrupting them—or becoming the 301st ladder-related fatality of the year—in the process.

Chapter Five

Adam

Adam hadn't posted anything on his Instagram account for a month. He hadn't thought much about it, since he hadn't done a photo shoot since before they'd left Boulder.

No, that was a lie. He had thought about it. In the wee hours of the night, when he couldn't sleep, when he put on the glamorous films from the forties and fifties that his grandmother had loved, and watched the way the light flickered on the living room wall more than he watched the films themselves, he thought about it.

He thought about what it felt like to see the world through the lens of his camera. How he could write or rewrite the story of any scene just by what he focused on and where he cropped the image.

How he could document the way a feeling or certain fall of light changed a person's face entirely.

He missed it so much it made his chest tight and his stomach hurt.

But he couldn't let himself think about it in the light of day, because if he did he'd question every choice he had made.

Now, he opened his account, ignored the notifications of friends and followers asking where he was, considered looking at Mason's account and instantly rejected the idea, then uploaded a picture of the tangle of Christmas lights he'd taken before ascending the ladder, and posted a call for help.

Hello, friends! I've been busy moving house with my daughter, but here I am, and I'd love your help. If anyone is in the Garnet Run, Wyoming area and has fairy lights to spare—any type—I could really use them. My daughter and I are working on a Christmas project. I'll post pics when it's done!

Four days later, life having driven the post completely from his mind, he arrived home from work to what appeared to be a bag of trash in his driveway. Irritated at whatever neighbor had decided to dump their garbage here, he got out of the car, muttering loudly, picked up the trash bag between two fingers, and moved to deposit it on the curb.

Then he saw the note taped to the side of the bag.

Hi, Adam. Big fan of your work. My mom had these in her garage and hasn't used them for years but they still work. Good luck with your Christmas project, and welcome to Wyoming!
—Matt

Tears filled Adam's eyes. The bag had four neatly coiled strands of lights that, to be fair, did look as though they'd spent more than a few years in a garage. Still, they were lights and Gus wanted lights, and Adam couldn't believe that someone he'd never met had taken the time to drop them off for him.

"Are you okay?"

Adam started. Wes stood in the shadows to his left, hands shoved in his pockets. Adam hadn't even noticed him approach.

"Hi. Yeah. You scared me."

"You were standing outside, clutching a garbage bag, and crying. I got concerned."

There was a time in Adam's life when he would have tried to hide his tears; would've protested, *I wasn't crying.*

The world wasn't kind to the sensitive. Adam had learned that long ago. For years he'd believed that his feelings were too big, too deep, too trip wire reactive.

It hadn't helped that his father had fed him poison his whole childhood. Beliefs about boys and tears that were designed to shame him and change him, but had had the curious effect, in adulthood, of making him treasure his tears. Treat them as proof that he was a different man than his father was.

Adam opened the bag so Wes could look inside.

"Good. Thought it might be a severed head or something."

Adam looked at him in horror.

"Does that...happen?"

Wes blinked and shoved his hands in the pockets of his jeans.

"No. I... Bad joke. Sorry."

"Oh."

They stood in silence for a moment and Adam realized it was the first time he'd seen Wes outside in the daylight—well, twilight, and he *was* lurking in the shadows. Adam said, "Do you want to help me put them up?" at the same time as Wes said, "Guess I better get home."

Then they both said "Oh" in unison.

Before Wes could turn away, though, Gus burst out the front door, River close on her heels.

"Wes, Wes!" she shouted, and threw herself at him.

"Oof," Wes said, but caught her handily.

He didn't seem to know what to do with her, though, so he held her in the air for a moment, then set her down on the ground and patted the top of her head, like a friendly monster in an animated film.

"What's that?" she asked, and dove into the trash bag.

"Good thing it *wasn't* a severed head," Adam said under his breath.

Wes snorted.

"Oh, this is my sibling, River," Adam said.

River had a way of standing so still and quiet that you could forget they were there. Adam had no doubt it was a survival tool, but he felt guilty every time it worked on him.

"River, this is Wes. He lives over there."

Wes and River shook hands and nodded at each other—two quiet, self-contained people reaching out of their containment to make reluctant contact.

Gus pulled lights out of the bag and tugged on Wes' jacket.

"Can we please go borrow your ladder to hang the lights?"

"Ladder's still here from last time." Wes pointed at it leaning against the side of the house.

"Oh." Gus sounded disappointed, but then she rallied and asked with perfect innocence, "Well then can we please go to your house to borrow something else?"

Adam snorted and River quirked a smile—Adam had filled them in on Gus' fascination with Wes' house. Wes just cocked his head and said, "What do you want to borrow?"

Gus thought about that, but honesty won out and she sighed.

"Nothing. I just wanna look at everything."

And Wes, whether because he was desperate to get back inside or because he honestly was a saint who didn't mind Gus' intrusion, said, "Okay."

The minute they got inside, Gus made a beeline for the basement and Adam bolted after her before she accidentally pulled bottles of chemicals down on her head or something.

The basement glowed with an eerie green light and for a moment, everything the neighbors had said about Wes echoed through his mind.

Gus had frozen in her tracks and was staring at the far wall of the basement, where glass jars on staggered shelves, with tubes protruding from them, contained the glow. Jars full of fireflies was all Adam could compare it to. He remembered that long ago summer when Marina had trapped them in her hands and put them in jars she'd carry around like night-lights against the coming dark.

Adam had thought it was the most beautiful thing he'd ever seen—like stars brought down to earth—until he realized that with the lid on the fireflies died, their beautiful glow darkened forever.

He'd cried when he found the first jar. Marina had been flippant. There would be more that night and they could just collect another jar. His father had been scornful. But Adam had never intentionally killed another thing again.

"What is it?" Gus asked, awed.

"I don't know."

"They're bacteria with luciferase enzyme and luciferin substrate," Wes said from behind them. "Fed on methane. It mimics naturally occurring bioluminescence."

"Whoa," Gus said worshipfully. She got quite close, then turned to Wes. "Can I touch it?"

"You can touch the jar."

She put her hand on it, then held her hand behind it so the glow traveled up her arm.

"Can you make anything glow?" she asked.

"Theoretically, yes," Wes said.

The basement was set up like a laboratory and Adam peered at Wes in the dim, virid light, imagining him as a Victor Frankenstein type, all moody eyes, sharp cheekbones, and ill-fated passion for creating life.

Ill-fated or no, Wes looked much more at ease in

his house than he had outside. His hands were out of his pockets, his anxious, darting glance had been replaced by an intent focus, and his words seemed to come easier.

"What are these?"

Gus moved to pick up a nonglowing jar on the table, and Wes and Adam both lurched toward her.

"Honey, don't touch things without asking," Adam said, taking the jar from her before she could drop it by accident.

However, when something inside it *moved*, Adam very nearly dropped it himself.

"Oh, god, what *are* they?"

Wes took the jar from him and cradled it to his chest protectively.

"Leeches."

Adam's stomach lurched.

"Like, uh, blood-sucking…bugs, leeches?"

"Leeches aren't bugs. They're in the worm family," Wes said matter-of-factly.

"Do they really suck blood?" Gus asked with fascinated glee. "Like vampires?"

"Well, not like vampires," Wes said mildly. "Because vampires aren't real."

Gus considered him. "You know everyone says *you're* a vampire."

"I know. And a werewolf."

He winked at her, then howled.

Adam started, but Gus laughed and then joined in the howls.

"Darren and Rose McKinnon said witch," Adam added.

Wes nodded sagely.

"Yeah, that too. I'm a vampire-werewolf hybrid who practices witchcraft and worships Satan. I'm extremely busy."

Adam laughed.

"Okay, but seriously. What's up with the snakes and spiders and leeches?"

Wes carefully set the jar of leeches down with a little pat, like the one he'd given Gus earlier.

"I like them," he said simply. "I've always liked them. They're fascinating."

He trailed a finger over an aquarium that Adam now saw contained several lizards.

"Everyone likes fuzzy things like dogs and cats. No one asks them why. But tarantulas are fuzzy and people find them terrifying. They love butterflies but they think leeches are disgusting. People kill totally harmless snakes all the time because they're scared of them."

He reached into the aquarium and one of the lizards—a small black one with an orange back—scampered up on his hand.

"But if people spent as much time with lizards and snakes as they did with dogs and cats, they'd realize how amazing they are. They have personalities too. All animals do."

Adam edged closer to Wes. The lizard was very beautiful. It flicked its tiny tongue out like it was tasting Wes' thumb.

He could acknowledge the beauty of the lizards, but the thought of that tarantula still filled him with utter horror.

"I don't mean to be scared of them," Adam said softly. "But isn't it, like, human nature?"

"No," Wes said. "Wolves are a threat to humans too, and anyone confronted with them would be afraid of them, but we don't naturally jump back from dogs because of it. We learn to fear snakes and spiders because we only encounter them in threatening contexts. By surprise in nature, or as villains in kids' movies. The way they move is unfamiliar, so we find it creepy."

He was watching the lizard fondly.

"But if we grew up in a culture where everyone had snakes and tarantulas as pets, we would be much less afraid of them. It's considered strange to have a pet rat, but normal to have a pet hamster. They're both in the Cricetidae family. But we think one is cute and one is horrible."

"Let me guess," Adam said. "You think rats are cute."

"Not especially. But I acknowledge that it's merely convention that makes people think they're less cute than hamsters."

He looked at the jar on the table.

"Leeches are much cuter than hamsters," he said.

Adam laughed, until it was clear Wes wasn't kidding.

"Can I hold a leech?" Gus asked.

Wes said, "If you do, it'll bite you and suck your blood a little. Are you okay with that?"

Adam gaped.

Gus asked, "Will it hurt?"

"Not really."

Gus shrugged. "Okay."

"Um, sorry, *not* okay. I would really prefer my daughter doesn't hold anything guaranteed to *suck her blood*."

"Well, I suppose it's not guaranteed—" Wes began.

"No. Nope. Thanks, but no."

"We have plenty to spare," Wes said mildly. Then, "You can hold Ludwig. He doesn't suck blood."

Wes held up the lizard that had scampered up his arm and onto his shoulder.

Gus nodded and held out her hand. She stroked the small lizard's back and giggled with delight when it ran onto her wrist.

"Gus isn't scared of them," Adam said.

"No." Wes cast a fond, respectful look at Gus.

"Wes, what do you *do*?" Adam asked. "Besides being a vampire-werewolf hybrid who practices witchcraft and worships Satan, of course."

Wes' blue eyes were intense as he spoke.

"I'm working to create a viable sustainable natural alternative to electric light," he said intently. "It's a huge problem, both in terms of unnecessary energy output and lack of access to necessary energy. Lighting accounts for twenty percent of worldwide energy used every year, so a natural alternative would cut down on our general energy usage. Electric light pollution spoils rural areas and scares animal populations out of their natural habitats, which can change entire ecosystems over time, so a natural alternative would be less disruptive. And urban neighborhoods that are primarily lower-earning people of color are severely underserved by cities' infrastructures, so they have a lack of electric streetlights, which makes the areas less safe and more susceptible to crime. A natural alternative to electric light could be more accessible for neighborhoods of that sort. If I can find a way to create this bioluminescent light, it could be used everywhere. Anywhere."

His eyes glowed with purpose.

"Holy crap," Adam said. "You really are a super-hero."

Chapter Six

Wes

Adam Mills arrived at Wes' doorstep looking harassed.

Since Adam had called him a superhero two nights before, Wes had carried around a feeling he didn't recognize. A spacious, fizzy sensation that made his head feel a bit light and the corners of his mouth turn up.

"I need to ask you a huge favor," Adam said, grimacing. "It's Gus' turn to do a show-and-tell at school, and all she'll talk about is wanting to bring, er, Bettie."

Adam shuddered when he uttered the tarantula's name, but Wes was touched. If Gus brought Bettie in to school and talked about why she was interested in her, she could convince a whole classroom of kids that tarantulas were lovely, fascinating creatures, and nothing to be afraid of.

"So," Adam said, "I need you to talk her out of it."

"Huh?"

"Yeah, just tell her Bettie doesn't like to ride in cars or something, maybe. Whatever you want. I can bring her by, or you could pop over. Whatever's easiest for you. I'm really sorry."

He ran a hand through his silky dark blond hair, and it settled in a messy fall around his face.

"It's just, when Gus gets fixated on something, it's nearly impossible to get her off it. You really have to replace it with another fixation instead." He seemed to be half talking to himself. "Anyway, I'm sorry to put you on the spot, but can you?"

"Can I talk her out of it?"

"Yeah."

"Or she could just take Bettie to school," Wes offered.

He had Adam's full attention now.

"Oh, no. No, no, that's not necessary. Nope. No worries."

Adam swallowed hard when he was scared, and his eyes darted around.

Wes couldn't believe what he was about to offer. But with each passing day he thought about Adam Mills more.

"I could go. With her. If she wants."

Adam blinked up at him. His eyes were a bluish-grayish color that reminded Wes of the Pacific Ocean on smoggy days.

"Can you *do* that?" He immediately flushed. "Oops, sorry. I didn't mean. Um."

There was a childish wonder to Adam that delighted Wes. He imagined it was probably where Gus got her own sense of wonder and curiosity, even if hers was for different topics.

"Will the sun burn me to a crisp, you mean?"

Adam laughed nervously, but he bit his lip and

looked up at Wes like he really would like to know the answer.

Wes leaned closer. Usually, Adam was energy in motion—one eye on Gus, the other on the ground in front of him to make sure he didn't trip.

But now Wes had his full attention. He looked into Adam's stormy eyes and took in the way his pupils dilated and his lashes swept downward. The way his mouth softened and parted slightly.

And he said, very seriously, "I'm willing to chance it."

Adam snorted and then looked sheepish.

"Sorry," he muttered.

"I'm not a vampire," Wes said mildly. Then, in his best Bela Lugosi voice, "I am a daywalker."

Adam's eyes got wide and Wes relented.

"Do you believe in vampires?" he asked.

"No!" Adam said very quickly. Too quickly. "Not really." He scuffed the stoop with the toe of his worn sneaker. "I don't know. It's just as possible as anything else, isn't it? No, no, never mind. Forget I said that."

He rolled his eyes at himself.

Wes thought about it. Adam's statement seemed absurd on the face of it, yes. But Wes hadn't gotten where he was today by dismissing ideas without thinking about them just because they sounded impossible.

"Leeches and lampreys feed on blood. So do some bats. Mosquitoes and fleas do too, and bedbugs. The oxpecker is a bird that eats bugs off oxen, then drinks blood from the wounds they created. Oh, and there's a finch that lives in the Galápagos that drinks blood from the booby bird. So, the blood-drinking part isn't unreasonable. It's really the immortality that's the sticking point. And the transforming others into a different creature through their bite. But I suppose those things could just be part of the mythos, not the biology."

Adam was watching him with a strange look. Usually, Wes hated being looked at. But Adam's attention didn't make him squirm.

"You're very open-minded," Adam said.

Wes shrugged. "It's just science."

Adam regarded him in silence, like he'd forgotten why he'd come.

"So, show-and-tell," Wes prompted. "When is it?"

"Huh? Oh, Friday. We leave at 8:30."

"In the morning," Wes said.

"Yeah."

Adam just looked at him. Wes had been trying to make a joke, but it had fallen flat.

"Okay," he said, and moved to shut the door, embarrassed.

"Thank you!" Adam called.

Wes watched him walk across the street, arms wrapped around himself against the cold.

He watched him and wondered what Adam would think if he knew Wes had just offered to leave Knockbridge Lane in the daylight for the first time in four years.

Early Friday morning, the ancient alarm clock that Wes had found in the basement and plugged in for the first time jerked him awake with violent beeps.

Banana chirped with displeasure at the unusual interruption, shoved her face under the blanket, and curled back up with Janice, looking more like a grouchy cat than a raccoon.

Wes wished he could curl back up with them. His nocturnal schedule was usually aligned with the raccoons', but today Wes dragged himself out of bed and into the shower. He couldn't remember the last time he'd gotten up before 2:00 p.m.

But that disruption to his schedule paled in comparison to the larger disruption. Westley Mobray was about to leave his house and go to a school full of people—full of *children*, no less—in the daylight, where anyone could look at him.

The mind reeled.

Wes wasn't agoraphobic. He didn't get panic attacks in crowded places, nor was it precisely fear he felt at the prospect of going to them. What he absolutely, positively hated was being looked at. Feeling as though he was being observed.

And because of that, he had a habit of trying to make himself invisible in scenarios when people would observe him. This resulted in a sensation of being alienated from his own body. Little by little as he stood there, pieces of him would begin to feel wrong. The arm closest to people would go all strange—like it had no function. Then perhaps the legs he stood on. Then a shoulder.

Until, after a while, he felt like a mass of whirling energy trapped in a strange and clumsy form that became a prison. When people looked at the prison, or needed it to function, it became bigger and clumsier and less effectual.

And then, all Wes wanted was to disappear.

It had begun the year he was fifteen. The year the whole world had seemed to be observing him. And it had never gone away. For the next three years he'd been forced to capitulate to social conventions because he was living in his parents' home. But once he moved out, he had the freedom to eschew those conventions and avoid people as he pleased.

With each passing year of doing so, he'd found it increasingly unpleasant to attend the social functions that other people seemed to navigate with ease.

Now, with no one to dictate his schedule or police his habits, Wes was free to avoid the places and situations that made him feel distant from himself.

He had everything delivered, from groceries to laboratory equipment. During the day, when sensory stimulation and chance encounters with people were at their height, Wes slept. In the quiet, private darkness, he lived his life. He found places to do experiments and caught rodents for the snakes. He socialized online or via video chat; and conducted his meetings and conference appearances in the same way.

Wes had cultivated precisely the life he wanted.

And now he was breaking every barrier he'd put in place to take a tarantula to a little girl's school.

Chapter Seven

Adam

Adam had spent the previous evening trying to temper Gus' excitement by reminding her that it was possible Wes might not show up.

"He will, Daddy. I know he will," Gus insisted, and Adam's heart clenched at the faith she already had in Wes—and at the knowledge that Wes might betray it.

He cursed himself one hundred times for not getting Wes' number so he could text to remind him.

By 7:00 a.m., he was a mess of nerves, gulping coffee and peering out the kitchen window at Wes' house, trying to see if he could spot a light or a TV on that might indicate his mysterious neighbor was awake.

It was impossible because of the paper covering all the windows.

"God, he's so weird," Adam muttered to himself as he poured another cup of coffee. "And hot," he added, regrettably honest with himself when he'd had very little sleep—which he had, the night before, waking at 2:00 a.m. convinced Wes would be a no-show, then watching a loop in his mind of all the times Mason had disappointed him or let Gus down.

"Why do I think he's so hot?"

Wes Mobray was strange and awkward and lived in a hellscape of a haunted house crawling with things that Adam didn't even wish to think about.

He was also kind and generous and obviously brilliant. He took Gus' interests seriously and didn't treat her like a kid. He loved animals that most people thought were creepy and was gentle with them. His blue eyes were warm and honest and when he smiled it made Adam want to smile.

"Welp, I guess that's why."

"Why what, Daddy?"

Gus wandered into the kitchen rubbing her eyes, wearing jeans, one sock, and her pajama top.

"Why you're the greatest kid in the world."

Gus rolled her eyes, but smiled a little, and Adam brushed her soft blond hair back from her face. She had a spot at the back of her head that was always knotted from sleeping on it and his heart swelled with tenderness whenever he saw it.

"Can I have waffles?" she asked, leaning into his touch.

"Yeah. I'll make them while you go put on a shirt and another sock."

She trudged out of the kitchen and Adam popped a frozen waffle into the toaster.

Absently, he added *Learn how to cook* to his ever-expanding list of things to do.

When the waffle popped up and Gus wasn't back yet, Adam nibbled on it absently and put another one in for her.

Adam was combing Gus' hair as she ate her waffle when the doorbell rang.

"He's here; he's here!" she shouted, and jumped up, knocking over the syrup jug.

Adam dove for it and got a handful of syrup for his trouble, but did save the jug from rolling to the floor.

He heard Gus open the door and Wes' quiet voice, but couldn't make out what he said.

"Hi," Adam called from the kitchen. "Be right there."

He washed his hands, cast a glance at the table and decided to leave the dishes for later, and went to greet Wes.

He had forgotten that for the duration of this outing, Wes equaled Wes and Bettie. He caught one glance of the tarantula in her carrier and decided that actually the dishes absolutely needed to be cleared from the table this very instant.

Adam deposited sticky dishes into the sink one at a time, taking deep breaths and saying to himself over and over again, *It's in a box; it can't hurt you.*

When he couldn't stall a moment longer, he steeled himself and went into the foyer. Wes stood there by himself, staring into space.

"Gus went to get something," he said when Adam approached. "I put a covering on her."

He held up the carrier that held Bettie, now draped with a pillowcase.

"Oh god, thank you," Adam said. "I'm so sorry. I know she's just a spider being a spider, but I'm terrified of her."

"I understand," Wes said simply.

He was wearing brown corduroy pants and a rust-colored wool sweater under a navy wool peacoat. He looked warm and touchable (tarantula aside), and Adam found himself wondering what it would feel like to run his hand up Wes' back. Feel his warmth through the softness of the fabric.

Gus skidded into the hallway holding her favorite accessories: a khaki explorer-style jacket that was a million times too big for her and a beekeeping hat with a veil of netting that covered her face.

She stuffed them in her backpack and announced, "Ready!"

Adam smiled. "My little naturalist."

Gus rolled her eyes because she thought *naturalist* sounded tame, but it was Adam's joke with himself, as when Gus was younger, she'd refused to wear any clothing, running around the house naked, and he'd called her his little naturist.

Adam buckled his seat belt and Wes slid in beside him, Bettie on his lap. Adam gulped.

"Um. Any chance Bettie can sit in the back seat, because if she gets out in the car, I will crash and kill us all."

Gus giggled, but Wes must've heard the mounting tension in his voice because he solemnly placed Bettie on the back seat and then rested his elbow on the armrest between their seats, blocking any potential spider entry point.

Adam silently melted.

They got to school without incident—spider or

vehicular—and Gus ran over to Abel, whom she'd described as having friend potential.

Adam turned to Wes to thank him again for going to all the trouble of coming here today, but Wes wasn't walking with him. He was standing, pressed to the side of the car, eyes wild.

"Hey. You okay?" Adam said softly, approaching on the non-tarantula side.

"Yes," Wes said, though he clearly was not. Then, "I don't go many places."

Adam almost made a flippant, unthinking comment, like *Me neither, since I had a kid* or *Not many places to go around here anyway.* But he quashed the knee-jerk impulse to defuse the awkwardness he felt and really looked at Wes.

Wes wasn't being flippant. Wes didn't seem to ever be anything but completely genuine, in fact, except on the rare occasions he attempted a joke. He was holding himself completely still and his eyes looked like he was elsewhere.

Adam touched him very lightly on the shoulder. When he didn't recoil, Adam let his hand rest there.

"How come?" he asked.

Wes looked down at him, his blue eyes unsure.

"I don't like people looking at me. It makes me feel very…strange."

Adam waited for more but no more was forthcoming and there wasn't really time now to ask all the questions he wanted to.

Instead, he squeezed Wes' shoulder and said,

"Well, there are at least two people here who think your brand of strange is pretty awesome."

Wes blinked at him.

"Uh, me and Gus, I meant," Adam clarified, feeling very corny.

"I knew who you meant," Wes said softly. "Thanks."

Gus ran over to them and bounced in place. Adam wondered, for the four-thousandth time, if he had ever in his life possessed that much energy.

"Come on, come on!"

Gus grabbed Adam's left hand and Wes' right hand and tugged them toward the school. Wes looked startled, but let himself be led.

Adam caught his eye as they were dragged, like a vee of geese, into the flock of children entering the building. He raised his eyebrows in question and Wes gave him a slight nod.

As they made their way down the hallway to Gus' second grade classroom, Adam was struck with the memory of walking Gus into her first day of kindergarten. She'd held his and Mason's hands just this way, but had been so tiny she practically dangled between them.

Mason had been flustered, wanting to find the right room and wondering aloud about the school, while Adam had worked hard to hold back tears at the thought of his baby going to school like such a big kid.

Gus had looked up at Mason and smiled and he'd been too distracted to notice. Then she'd looked at Adam and he'd smiled at her big enough for both her parents. She had grinned, showing the gap where one of her front teeth had fallen out the week before, and Adam had felt a physical jolt of love so strong he couldn't believe he could function after.

How was a parent to survive feelings of such enormity? How could he go about his daily life when another person held his heart in her tiny hand?

It had never gone away, that feeling, though Adam now fancied himself a bit better at functioning despite it.

Now, as if she shared his memory, Gus looked up at him and grinned just as she had that day more than two years ago. Adam smiled back at her and winked.

Then, Gus turned her head and looked up at Wes.

As if he felt her eyes on him, Wes looked down at her and smiled.

Adam's eyes filled with tears he quickly blinked away. Wes was practically a stranger—at most, a neighbor. Adam had no business expecting anything from him, no matter how damn wonderful he was being. Expecting things from people was how you ended up disappointed, foolish, and heartbroken.

Gus pulled them into her classroom and over to her teacher.

"Ms. Washington, Ms. Washington, this is my dad, and this is Wes, and that's Bettie. She's my show-and-tell."

She pointed to the covered cage Wes held.

"That's great, August," she said brightly, bending down. "Is Bettie a hamster? A guinea pig?"

Gus reached out and before she could unceremoniously whip the pillowcase off, surprising Ms. Washington with a tarantula in the face, Adam grabbed Gus and threw an affectionate arm around her.

He gestured Ms. Washington away slightly and made a crawling spider with his fingers. Her eyes got very wide and she raised one elegant eyebrow. Adam inclined his head. *I'm afraid so*, his gesture said.

Without missing a beat, Ms. Washington said, "Why don't you sit down, August, and your dads can wait in the back with—er—Bettie?"

Gus skipped off to her desk without correcting Ms. Washington.

From the back of the room, Adam could see how small Gus was compared to the other kids. He'd been small for his age too.

She was nearly bouncing in her seat, and she kept looking over her shoulder at them. She waved at Wes and he waved back—a tiny movement of his hand at his side.

Wes leaned in. "They're so…little," he mused.

"Yeah, isn't it weird? You don't feel little as a kid. You're always the biggest you've ever been."

Adam wanted to ask Wes what he'd been like as a child. Had he been an amateur scientist, fascinated by dinosaurs and insects, as Adam imagined him? Had he always been so quiet, so self-contained? Or had that happened later—the result of his interactions with the world rather than the cause of them?

When it was time for Gus' show-and-tell, she ran to the front of the room, pulling on her explorer jacket and beekeeping hat as she went.

"My show-and-tell is named Bettie. She's a tarantula!"

Gus was grinning, her eyes wide with excitement. This was the moment Adam had been dreading. Not all of her classmates were going to be pleased with this addition to their number, and he didn't want to see the light in Gus' eyes dim with their rejection.

A few of the kids exchanged scared looks, but many leaned forward, interested.

"Should I go up?" Wes murmured.

"I think so."

Wes strode through the aisles of desks, looking like a giant in a land of Lilliputians. He stood next to Gus, awaiting her command.

Gus told the class a few tarantula facts that she'd read about in the insect compendium Adam had brought home from the thrift store, and more that Wes had clearly told her. Wes softly corrected her pronunciation of *arthropod*, and then it was time.

Adam pinched his arm, telling himself that Bettie was all the way across the room. She'd have to get past twenty second-graders to make it to him. Still, he let his eyes unfocus as the pillowcase came off Bettie's cage.

It did help a little to think of her as Bettie, rather than a spider. Bettie lived with Wes. Wes held her in his hand. That meant it was all okay.

Adam was concerned that his brain had begun to equate *Wes* with *Everything is okay*.

Wes held Bettie's cage up so everyone could see. Then he told them he would take her out, but they had to be very quiet and very still. His voice was low and soft, and not a child moved or made a sound as he opened the Plexiglas door and gently picked up Bettie.

He cooed to her and she stayed in his cupped palm. Adam focused on Wes' face, pretending his hand didn't even exist.

From across the room, as if he could feel Adam's gaze on his face, Wes' eyes snapped to his.

Wes' expression was subtler than Gus', but Adam saw in his clean, rough features the same joy, the same excitement, and the same desire to share that fascination with others.

It was beautiful. He was beautiful.

The children asked questions and Wes answered every one. He told them what Bettie ate, when she slept, and if she spun webs. When he told them that tarantulas shot silk from their feet, one of the boys called, "She's like Spiderman!" and Wes said, "Spiderman's like her." The boy looked like his mind had been blown.

For all their fascination with Bettie, the kids were clearly nervous when Wes asked if anyone wanted to touch or hold Bettie. No one raised their hand. Gus held out her cupped palms and Wes placed Bettie into them.

Once they'd seen Gus touch Bettie and live to tell the tale, another girl's hand went up, and Gus put the tarantula into her palm very carefully. "Don't move, even when she moves," Gus told her seriously, as Wes had once told her.

Once everyone who wanted to had held or touched

Bettie, under Gus' watchful eye, Ms. Washington called an end to show-and-tell. The class applauded and Gus stood, grinning from ear to ear.

As Wes and Adam walked out of the classroom and through the empty hallways, Adam touched Wes' arm, the wool of his sweater as soft as he'd imagined.

"Thank you," Adam said. "Thank you so much for doing this. It meant the world to Gus. And to me."

Wes looked down at Adam and seemed at a loss for words. Clearly the experience in the classroom had meant something to him.

"They weren't scared of her," he said.

"Kids are brave. They mostly haven't learned to be afraid of things yet."

The lucky ones, anyway. The ones who didn't have fear fed to them at home, where fear should never be.

"Like you said. I think we learn to be scared and then once we're scared we hate the things we fear because it's easier than working on our fear."

Wes glanced at Bettie's cage, once more covered with the pillowcase.

Adam reached over and very slowly, breathing deeply to ground himself, pulled the fabric away.

He felt his heart start to beat faster, Bettie's movements triggering a long-held disgust deep within him. He let his eyes go a bit unfocused so he could see her through a haze. This was Bettie. Wes' beloved pet. She was an animal, like a cat or a squirrel.

He watched her for a few moments, and thought neutral thoughts about her. He didn't even notice he'd stepped back until Wes moved to put the pillowcase back over the cage.

Wes' blue eyes were warm and soft and he stepped toward Adam.

Adam's heart was beating fast now for an entirely un-spider-related reason. Wes' mouth looked lush and soft and his shaved hair looked like velvet.

Wes pressed one broad shoulder into Adam's and said solemnly, "Thank you."

Chapter Eight

Wes

"You did what?!" His friend's voice was at least an octave higher than usual. Wes had just told Zachary about Gus' show-and-tell. "But you mean an actual, human child?"

"Yes, a *Homo sapiens* child."

Zachary snorted. His friend was one of the only people who could tell when he was joking.

Zachary only lived four miles away, but they mostly spoke on the phone or via chat. Once in a while, Zachary would FaceTime him to show him something, but he didn't seem to mind that Wes preferred they never meet in person.

"How did the Halloween decorating go?" Wes asked, realizing Halloween had come and gone without his notice.

"Excellent. I won. Obviously."

Zachary lived on Casper Road, and every year the residents competed in a neighborhood Halloween decorating contest. Kids from all around the county went there and trick-or-treated. Zachary took it extremely seriously, not caring about the children or the neighborhood—only about the trophy that was bestowed on the house with the best decorations.

He'd won every year he had lived on Casper Road and approached the Halloween season with all the planning and dedication with which he approached his architectural blueprints—if a bit more of a competitive spirit.

"Congratulations. I'm sure you terrified the human children."

"Oh, to be sure." Wes could hear the smile in his voice. "And I'm already planning for next year. It's going to be truly epic."

"I can do lighting," Wes offered absently.

In the past he'd created some eerily glowing effects for Zachary's windows.

"Definitely."

Zachary began to outline his plans for the next year's decorations, and Wes tuned out as he checked the biogas generator. It was an accepted tenet of their friendship that both of them had free rein to wax enthusiastic about their niche pursuits, and either of them were welcome to stop listening when they lost interest. It worked for them.

When he finished with the biogas generator and went into the basement to feed the lizards, Zachary was describing something made of wire and silicone that sounded like it might be a skeleton.

His phone beeped with an incoming call.

"Hang on a sec, Zachary."

Wes looked at his phone. The incoming call was from Adam Mills. Wes' heart sped up at the sight of

his name. They'd exchanged phone numbers after
Gus' show-and-tell, Adam adorably flustered and
making up reasons why it was good for neighbors
to have one another's contact information, but Wes
hadn't thought anything would come of it.

"Hello?"

"Wes, thank god. I'm so glad you answered. I
mean, hi, hello, it's Adam. Mills. From across the
street. How are you?"

Though it was the first time he'd heard Adam's
voice on the phone, somehow Wes felt as though they
did this all the time—Adam calling, enthusiastic or
in a hurry; Wes answering, waiting for the infusion
of sparkle that Adam's next words might bring.

"What's up?"

"Okay, I'm so damn sorry to ask you for another
favor, but I'm at work and my damn car won't start.
River's with Gus, but they have to leave in half an
hour to meet the vet at the cat shelter so they can't
stay with her. Is there any way you would be able to
pop over to my house and stay with Gus until I can
get home? It shouldn't be more than an hour or so."

"Go over to your house," Wes echoed.

"And hang out with Gus, yeah. Wes, are you
there?"

He'd thought he was speaking, but apparently not.

"I don't know what to do?"

"With Gus? No worries, just watch a movie, or
you can read a book and tell her to play in her room.
Really, it's just so she's not alone."

If he were to stop and think about it, Wes would

realize that Adam and Gus were the first people outside his family to ask him for anything in years.

Once, he had been someone people asked things of. Asked far too much of. But when he pulled into himself, he shed those connections like a snakeskin.

He waited to see if the request would feel suffocating, as requests once had, but all he felt was a warm tingle in his stomach. Excitement at the prospect of seeing Adam again.

"Okay."

"Really?! Oh, god, thank you so much, Wes. You're saving my life, seriously."

"Should I go now?"

"If you don't mind, that would be wonderful."

"Okay."

He hung up and switched over to the other call.

"Zachary, I have to go."

"Oh. Okay."

"I have to go watch a human child."

"The kid from across the street again? You never told me if her dad is attractive. Wes. Westley. Is he hot? Wes, hey!"

"Bye, Zachary."

River answered the door with their coat already on.

"Thanks, Wes," they said. "I'd stay, but the vet is coming by to look at one of the kittens and I have to be there to let her in."

"That's understandable. I hope the kitten is okay."

River smiled. "Me too."

Gus ran at Wes the second he got inside.

"Wes!"

"Hi, Gus. What are you up to?"

Gus shrugged. "Me and River were building a fort, but I'm bored of that. Can we do science?"

"Building a fort is science. It's physics."

Gus cocked her head like she was considering that. "Oh. Well can we do *other* science?"

Wes didn't know much about kids, but as Adam had pointed out the other day, he had *been* one. He could certainly give Gus what he wished someone had given him when he was her age.

"Want to do some chemistry?"

Gus grinned and nodded enthusiastically.

Two and a half hours later, Adam walked into the kitchen looking exhausted. There were circles under his blue eyes, and his clothes were rumpled. Wes had the strongest urge to fold him in his arms. To press his thumbs to those dark circles as if he could erase them simply by noticing.

When Adam saw the state of the kitchen, his eyes widened. Wes had intended to clean things up before Adam returned, but had lost track of time. He'd been having such fun with Gus.

"Whoa."

"Daddy, we're doing science!" Gus announced.

"That's great, sweetheart," Adam said weakly.

"We were looking at some chemical reactions," Wes explained, hoping to distract from the mess.

"We made a volcano that erupted all over the place," Gus said, pointing with a grin and ruining any chance of a distraction. "And we made plastic out of milk!"

Adam raised an eyebrow at that, like he thought it was a child's whimsy.

"Milk contains casein molecules," Wes explained. "Proteins. A chain of casein monomers makes a polymer that can be molded, kind of like plastic."

"Wow, cool."

Adam's blond hair was messier than usual, as if he'd run his hands through it over and over in frustration, and Wes had the strangest urge to push it back from his face.

"You really saved us today," Adam was saying. "Do you wanna stay for dinner? I was just gonna make mac and cheese, but…"

Part of Wes itched to get back home where it was safe and private.

But he also felt a competing pull to stay. Suddenly, he dearly wanted to eat macaroni and cheese with Adam and Gus.

"Okay," he heard himself say to Adam for the second time that day.

"Yay!" Gus shouted and threw her arms around his waist.

Over gloppy orange macaroni and cheese, Gus regaled Adam in greater detail about their science projects and Adam told the harrowing tale of his car breaking down outside Matheson's Hardware. ("Charlie wanted to try and fix it himself and then when he couldn't, insisted on calling his friend to tow it.")

It mostly sounded nice to Wes, but Adam seemed embarrassed to have needed his boss' help.

Gus launched into a monologue about leeches and Adam turned a suspicious eye at Wes. Wes innocently ate another spoonful of macaroni and cheese, impressed that Gus remembered most of what he'd told her, and Adam's face fizzed into a smile.

Wes didn't notice he was staring into Adam's blue eyes until Gus said, *"Hello?!"*

Wes blinked. Adam cleared his throat, flustered, and said, "That's rude, sweetheart."

After dinner, Adam went to tuck Gus into bed and Wes looked around the kitchen at the mess they'd made. He could go home. Adam would understand. His critters were there, and his work. And the darkness, and the solitude.

Instead, Wes cleared the table and began to make order out of the chaos he'd created.

Chapter Nine

Adam

Adam was exhausted by the time Gus fell asleep. She'd been abuzz with excitement about her evening with Wes and had wanted to tell him everything she'd learned. It was sweet and wonderful and he'd wanted to press a mute button on her after about six minutes.

Finally, he trudged back to the kitchen to clean up, and pulled out his phone to send Wes a thank-you text.

But when he got to the kitchen, Wes was still there, and it was the mess that was gone.

The floor and countertops sparkled, and the dishwasher was humming.

Relief and gratitude consumed him. They never told you about this: the part where sometimes after a day of work and car trouble and kid wrangling, not having to do the dishes could bring you to tears.

Wes looked startled and held out a large hand quellingly.

"Hey. Oh. Hey," he stumbled.

"You cleaned up," Adam said, voice shaking.

"Well, yeah. I made the mess."

Adam nodded, because that was logical and also miraculous.

"Listen, I did something," Wes said, shoving a hand in his pocket and looking guilty.

Please don't be anything creepy, Adam begged the universe. *He's so great; please don't make me have to hate him*.

"I organized your dry goods," Wes said.

"My...dry goods."

Wes opened three cabinets, revealing perfectly ordered foodstuffs where once there had been a riot.

"I was cleaning up and it just kind of leaked into the cabinets," he went on. "I guess I lost track of time. I can put them back to the way they were if you want..."

Heat bloomed in Adam's chest. Wes was so damned adorable. This large, strong, recluse of a science genius had organized his pantry storage by... He stared at the cabinets, trying to parse the logic.

"Um. How did you arrange it?"

Wes blinked at him as if it were obvious.

"Alphabetically."

Adam didn't let himself laugh.

"Of course," he murmured.

And so it was, almonds to ziti.

"I'm gonna make a wild guess that you don't cook," Adam said.

"I cook. Quite a bit, actually."

They stared at each other. Adam pictured Wes in his own kitchen, reaching for ingredients filed alphabetically as he cooked a meal for himself and his coterie of critters.

"Thank you for cleaning up. And for, er, rearranging my dry goods."

They stood in awkward silence for a moment. Wes was gorgeous and kind and smart and incredibly weird, but in great ways. Once, Adam would have kissed him. He would have said, *Thanks for cleaning up. I want to kiss you. Whattaya say?*

But Adam's days of risking his heart were behind him. These days, he didn't go around falling for gorgeous, kind, smart, weird-in-great-ways men—especially ones who lived right across the street.

Did he?

Wes reached out a hand and his fingers hovered near Adam's shoulder.

"Your hair looks so soft," he murmured.

"You can touch it," Adam said, breath catching. "If you want."

He expected tentative fingertips, or the gentle *hush* of his hair being swept back.

But at his invitation, Wes slid his large hands into Adam's hair, massaging his scalp with strong fingers. An involuntary groan escaped Adam's lips and he let his head fall forward and rest against Wes' firm chest.

He could hear the steady thump of Wes' heart and closed his eyes. Wes rubbed at his scalp and combed through his hair, stopping here and there to untangle.

"Adam."

"Mmm-hmm."

But he didn't say anything else. Adam tipped his head up to look at Wes. His eyes were burning hot and he was looking down at Adam like he held something precious in his hands.

"Wes," Adam whispered. "Can I kiss you?"

There went the neighborhood.

Wes' hands moved from his hair to his face, gently—so gently—cupping his jaw. He nodded.

Adam stood on his tiptoes and brushed his lips against Wes' softly. Wes let him, so Adam kissed him again. Wes' hands remained gentle, but his breath caught.

Suddenly, Adam wanted him with a hunger he hadn't felt in years. He pressed against Wes, leaning in to deepen the kiss. Wes' mouth was hot, his kiss clumsy with desire, but so damn sincere. Adam lost himself in it.

The kiss burned hotter and hotter and Adam pressed closer, desperate to feel Wes' body. Finally, Wes' arms came around him, clutching him close, tight, exactly as he craved.

Adam felt wild. The desire for Wes coursed through him until he was nearly dizzy with it. It had been so long. So damn long since he'd gotten what he needed.

Even with Mason sex had never been their main compatibility. Mason had been all about experimentation and erotic novelty, where Adam had craved intimacy and intensity. But Adam felt an answering passion in Wes that made him dare to hope that maybe Wes' desires would match his own.

Flushed and so turned-on he could hardly think, Adam wrapped his arms around Wes' neck and gave himself over to the kiss. Wes slid his hands to Adam's ass and gave it a rough squeeze that had Adam's eyes rolling back in his head.

"Yes, yes, yes," he murmured into Wes' mouth.

He pressed Wes against the freshly washed countertop, getting as close as he could. He loved it like this—so entwined that there was no breath that wasn't shared, no movement of his partner's body he couldn't feel.

Wes grabbed him by the ass and picked him up, walking them out the kitchen, through the living room, and up the stairs. Adam pointed to his bedroom at the end of the hall, light-headed with desire.

Wes wasn't making a show of strength, which made it a thousand times hotter. He just wanted Adam in bed, *now.* When they got inside Adam's room, Wes tossed him onto the bed then closed the door.

"Is it okay?" he asked, gesturing down the hallway to where Gus slept.

Adam's heart melted at his concern and he nodded.

"She sleeps with a noise machine, and these are pretty thick walls."

He didn't mention that he'd forced River to test that fact with him when they'd first moved in, making his sibling stand in Gus' room while he made noise in his own. But he'd needed to know.

Wes' gaze heated as he approached the bed, towering over Adam.

"Good."

Adam knew in that moment that Wes was going to be exactly what he wanted. What he craved. The roughness, the intensity, the glorious ability to not have to take care of anything and trust that the other person would take your pleasure in hand.

He also knew in that moment why the neighbors had so many rumors that Wes was a vampire, werewolf, et cetera. Looming over Adam, cheeks flushed with desire, eyes dark with lust, he looked intimidating. Devastating. Potent. And completely focused on Adam in a way that took his breath away.

"Wes, I want you," Adam whispered, and he turned onto his stomach, looking back at Wes pointedly.

"Yeah?"

Wes sat on the edge of the bed and ran a hand up Adam's spine. The heat from his palm was searing.

"Yes! I want—"

But even though he was pretty sure his needs were echoed in Wes, it was hard to say them out loud.

Wes leaned close and spoke in his ear. His voice was a velvet growl.

"Tell me exactly what you want."

Adam whimpered. Shook his head. The words wouldn't come.

"Adam, tell me."

"I want you to have me. Completely. Take me apart."

With the words came the liquid fire of want.

Wes groaned and his hand tightened around the nape of Adam's neck.

"Yeah? Kinda…take charge?"

"Yes," Adam moaned.

"In charge, but not…mean?"

Adam was dizzy with the potency of this understanding. That was exactly what he wanted. Exactly what he needed.

"Yes, yes, please, Wes, yes."

Adam pressed his hips into the bed and shuddered at the contact. He was hard and swollen, exquisitely sensitive.

But Wes caught his hip and flipped him onto his back. He straddled his hips and pressed a hand to his chest, keeping him in place. Adam trembled, loving the warm pressure.

Wes kissed Adam's jaw, then moved to his neck. At the crook where his shoulder and neck met, he sucked, and Adam felt it in his bones. He shuddered and thrashed under Wes' touch.

"Are you sure you aren't secretly a vampire?" he teased, with the last of his wits.

"Maybe I am," Wes murmured against his skin.

Adam giggled and Wes smiled—an easy, warm smile that said *We are in this together. I got you*.

Then he pinched Adam's nipple through his shirt and made him squirm.

"Sensitive," Wes murmured, ghosting a kiss to his flushed cheekbone.

Adam had heard that his whole life, and not only in this context. It was true, either way.

Wes pushed his shirt up slowly, kissing the skin he revealed, until the shirt was around Adam's neck. Then he began to torment his nipples so exquisitely that Adam wondered if he could come from it. But each time he felt the pleasure begin to crest, Wes would switch sides.

Adam was desperate for more and he pulled Wes down on top of him. Wes devoured his mouth and settled into the space between Adam's legs. When their erections came into contact they both gasped.

Breathing each other's exhalations, they slowly began to move. Above him, Wes was fire and steel and laser-focused attention, and Adam threw his head back, overwhelmed by the magnitude of his want.

He didn't even realize he was begging until Wes said, "Okay."

Wes rolled Adam's hips up and ground them together, hard and slow. Adam shuddered as waves of pleasure tore at him. He cried out and Wes swallowed his cry along with his kiss.

Then it was a frenzy. Wes held him and thrust their hips together with perfect force. Adam tossed his head on the pillow helplessly.

"Need you, please," he begged, straining upward.

Wes bore down on him, chest rubbing over his sensitive nipples, and ground against him so perfectly Adam saw stars. The seam of Wes' jeans was catching the spot just beneath the head of his cock that always made him come ribbons, and he threw his head back and let Wes have him.

Wes' thrusts got harder and faster, then just as Adam thought he'd lose it, Wes backed off, leaving Adam panting and desperate.

When he thought he couldn't take it anymore, Wes cupped his cheek and said, "You're so beautiful."

Then he swiveled his hips, twisting and grinding down in a movement that sent sparks shooting up Adam's spine.

"Again," Adam begged.

Wes did it again and again until Adam was a sobbing mess. Only then did Wes kiss his wet cheeks, slide his hands under Adam's ass to lift him up, and press them together perfectly.

The pressure built and built until Adam thought he would scream, then he was coming in wracking waves of pleasure that tore sounds from his throat he didn't recognize.

Just as it began to ebb, Wes pinched his nipple and roared his own orgasm, and Adam tumbled back into pleasure.

The aftershocks left him twitching and gasping on the bed, and when Wes collapsed on top of him, kissing his neck softly, he moaned at the ghosts of pleasure.

"Oh my *god*, Wes," Adam groaned.

He looked over at Wes and saw tenderness in his eyes. A soft connectedness that he'd never seen before.

Wes smiled at him and began to say something, when a yell shattered the silence.

"Daddy! Daddy!"

Chapter Ten

Adam

It had only been a nightmare, but Gus' cries had been enough to disrupt the mood. When Adam got back to bed, Wes was fully clothed and standing at the window, looking out at the moon. Or his own house. Adam couldn't be sure.

"Hey," he said, uncertain of his reception. He imagined the shrieks of an eight-year-old weren't everyone's postcoital cup of tea.

"I should get home," Wes said, confirming his suspicions.

"Sure."

Adam tucked his hair behind his ears and walked out into the living room, looking for Wes' shoes.

"Sorry," Adam offered miserably when Wes stood at the door.

"For what?" Wes seemed genuinely puzzled.

"For…Gus? Interrupting?"

Wes shrugged and shook his head.

"Nightmares suck," was all he said. Then he stepped out into the night.

Adam had nothing to say to that, so he watched Wes give him a wave, then walk away home.

* * *

"We need more, Daddy," Gus lamented, looking up at the house.

Adam thought the Christmas lights they had so far looked good, but he couldn't deny they were still sparse.

"Well, it is Saturday morning," Adam said, waggling his eyebrows.

"Oh, nooo," Gus groaned.

"Come on, it'll be great! There're sure to be lights."

"Okay, but we need a time limit." Gus tapped the black rubber watch she'd worn since before she was old enough to know what time was.

"Aw, you can't put a time limit on treasure hunting," Adam said, but he winked at her. "Fine, thirty minutes per stop."

Gus narrowed eyes the same blue as his own.

"Twenty," she offered.

"Deal."

Adam stuck out his hand and they shook on it.

"I'll grab snacks, you get dressed."

Estate sales were one of Adam's favorite things in the whole world. Mason had tolerated them but didn't have the same enthusiasm Adam did. Gus liked to pretend that it was torture to be dragged along, but Adam knew the truth.

She loved picking through the tangle of trash and treasure the same as he did. It was how she'd gotten her explorer jacket and her beekeeping hat, not to mention all her best wooden blocks and a trash can for her room that had a beetle hand-painted on it.

Adam had found his love for them by accident. Their elderly neighbor next door in Boulder had died, and her children hired a company to run a sale. Adam had gone over to offer his condolences to her daughter and instead found a new passion.

The world of estate sales was as particular as any, and as he went more often he learned the conventions of bargaining, of putting together a lot, of paying cash, of going on the last day of the sale for cut prices.

He also began to recognize many familiar faces at multiple sales. They were mostly, though not exclusively, white women in their fifties and sixties, and white men in their seventies, so he stood out.

But Adam had always stood out, so he was used to it.

Gus came crashing downstairs with several reusable totes on her arm.

"Ready!" she said, forgetting that she'd been feigning a lack of enthusiasm.

She skipped outside to the car and Adam followed her. His eyes were immediately magnetized to Wes' house and he shivered at the memory of his orgasm the night before.

How perfectly firm and gentle Wes had been. Brutal and caring. Adam shuddered again, hoping he wasn't flushing visibly.

"Daddy, let's invite Wes!"

"Oh, honey, Wes sleeps really late. It's only nine."

Gus pouted at Wes' house, and as if it saw her, the paper covering an upstairs window fluttered aside.

"Look, he's awake!" She pointed. "Unless that was one of the snakes," she mused.

"Oh god," Adam muttered.

"Let's ask. Can we please just ask?"

Adam really did want to see Wes. He wasn't proud of letting his kid do the dirty work for him, but he also wasn't above seizing the opportunities presented to him. Sometimes they were all you had.

"Well," he began.

"Yay!" Gus cried, sensing his imminent capitulation.

Then off she ran across the street, after exaggeratedly looking both ways.

Adam sighed and followed her, texting a warning to Wes as he went.

"You didn't ring more than once, did you?" Adam asked as he caught Gus up on the porch.

She blinked up at him. "Well. Twice."

"We've talked about this," Adam began, but before he could remind Gus, the door opened.

Wes was dressed and he was wearing sunglasses. He was holding a book and something that Adam, as a hardware store employee, really should've been able to identify, but could not.

"Hi," Wes said. And even though Adam couldn't see his eyes behind the sunglasses, somehow he knew Wes was looking right at him.

Gus bounced in place.

"Wanna come treasure hunting with us?" She held up the tote bags like they were a map where x marked the spot.

Adam opened his mouth to explain, but Wes said, "Yes."

"You *do*?" Gus sounded as surprised as Adam felt and Wes looked. But unlike him, his daughter knew when not to question a good thing. "Yay, come on!"

And then she grabbed his arm to pull him outside.

"Sweetie, he might need a minute."

Wes held up one finger and disappeared inside.

"Yay!" Gus crowed again, and hugged Adam.

Adam squeezed her tight and stroked her soft hair and tried to pinpoint why his heart was racing.

Excitement at spending time with this intriguing, lovely man? Yes.

But also…fear. In the space of two weeks, Gus already admired him. Already automatically included him in their plans.

And Adam—well, Adam knew what it was to fall fast and hard. He knew what it was to have a heart that gave itself away. And he knew what it was to have that heart treated without care.

You slept together one time! Don't turn a hot night into a lifelong commitment.

But then Wes came outside, navy blue peacoat perfectly showcasing his broad shoulders, mouth looking like sweet temptation, and all Adam could do was cross his fingers that this didn't end in devastation.

The first estate sale was a bust, but the second was gold. A farmhouse full of Western antiques and a two-story barn that was a picker's paradise. Or, in their case, paradise for an eight-year-old who fancied herself a scientist and an *actual* scientist who seemed to see possibility in everything.

Adam left them to rummaging through the tools, screws, and bits of twisted metal in the abandoned barn and wandered back into the house.

The joy of estate sale-ing for Adam didn't lie in buying. It lay in seeing someone's life laid out before you in objects and their arrangement. Imagining, as you ran reverent fingers over their belongings, the months, years, decades that assembled this collection in this configuration.

Each one was the museum of a life, and Adam was a happy tourist.

Though he wasn't a big buyer, there was one thing he always looked for: Royal China Jeanette ceramic pie plates printed with recipes. His grandmother had once had a whole set of them: apple pie, strawberry pie, rhubarb pie, pumpkin pie—each with a picture and recipe painted on them.

He didn't know what had happened to them when she died—for all he knew, the plates he'd once eaten cherry pie off of in her cozy kitchen had found their way into this very house.

He didn't find any, but he did find a French press for three dollars that he bought before going to find Gus and Wes in the barn.

"Daddy, Daddy, look!"

Gus ran toward him, her green Boulder Farmer's Market tote bulging.

She was holding a small aquarium with one pane of glass missing and her smile was radiant.

"Cool," he said, hoping it was the right response.

"Yeah, Wes says he has a piece of glass that will fit, and we can pox it."

"Epoxy," Adam murmured.

"And then I can fill it with whatever I want," she concluded triumphantly.

"Sounds great." The thing looked cheap enough, and he was always glad for Gus to have projects. "Let me just find the person to pay for it."

"Wes already gave me money and I bought it. And this stuff."

She opened her bag to reveal… Adam couldn't really tell what. A jumble of bits and pieces that no doubt made sense to his daughter. He'd just go through it later and make sure nothing was sharp.

"Well that was really generous of him. Did you say thank you?"

"Yes!"

Gus looked offended. Adam held up his hand and she gave him a high five.

"Where is Wes?"

Her eyes lit once more, and she pulled him to the barn entrance.

Wes was in the process of unearthing some kind of very rusty piece of equipment.

"Do you know what that is?" Adam asked.

Gus nodded sagely, ever delighted to be in the know.

"A trough."

"Like…for animal feed?"

"Wes said it's for algae," she explained graciously. Paused. Then said, "What's algae?"

With each passing year—no, month—Gus' questions challenged him more and more. Revealed all the things he didn't know. It was disturbing how often she asked him something that he'd lived his whole life not questioning, only to realize he wasn't sure enough of it to explain it to his kid.

"Algae's…um…a little plant that lives in the water? I think?"

Gus nodded. "We can google it."

Adam's heart swelled. This was what he always told her when he wasn't sure. Then they looked it up together. Some of his favorite moments with Gus were standing in the middle of wherever they were—the farmer's market, the drug store, a park—huddled over his phone, satisfying her curiosity and his desire to give her accurate information.

It had irked Mason. *She's three*, he'd say. *She doesn't need to know the genus and species. Just tell her it's a damn turtle.* Or, *She's five. You can tell her the sun revolves around the earth for all she'll care or remember.*

He hadn't meant it cruelly. He'd thought it was burdensome for Gus and a waste of time for Adam. He never understood that Adam was devoted to delivering the world to Gus in the most accurate way he could imagine. He'd never understood a lot of things about Adam.

But Adam *was* devoted to it. Because it was the right thing to do.

And because his own parents had given to him a world so warped by their own prejudices, beliefs, and convictions that he had spent a decade untangling it.

He would spend as long as it took googling every single goddamned thing in the world if it meant he never did that to Gus.

Wes made a triumphant noise, and the trough was free. When he looked up and saw Adam standing there, Wes smiled at him. A smile so automatic and sweet and happy at Adam's presence that it took Adam's breath away.

"What'd you find?"

Wes ran a palm over his shaved head the way he sometimes did when he explained things. It thrilled Adam that he knew that.

"Bioluminescence occurs naturally in microorganisms like dinoflagellates. I've been working with bacteria and methane gas, as you know."

Adam nodded, remembering the glowing green bottles.

"But I've been curious about the viability of individuals farming their own bioluminescent dinoflagellates. Pyrocystis fusiformis, probably."

Adam had understood only a few of the words that had just been spoken.

"You mean, um, you're gonna see if people can grow the bioluminescent algae themselves to, like, light their houses and stuff?"

"Oh, no," Wes said, smiling. "Algae are far too temporary a measure for replacing light sources. They only remain viable for a few weeks and then they need to be replaced or divided. This would just be an experiment for me. Just for fun."

"Sure, fun," Adam echoed. "Er, what is algae, precisely?"

"Photosynthetic, mainly aquatic eukaryotic organisms ranging from microscopic single-celled forms to multicellular forms one hundred feet or more long. They lack the true roots, stems, and leaves that other plants have, as well as nonreproductive cells in their reproductive structures. But there is dissent about the exact definition, because the word describes such a large and diverse group."

Adam blinked.

"And in layman's terms that would mean…?"

Wes cocked his head. "Oh. They're organisms that live in the water and can be as tiny as one cell or as big as kelp and seaweed."

"Nailed it," Adam congratulated himself. "Uh, is that gonna fit in the car?"

Wes seemed not to have considered that.

It turned out that the trough did fit, with some aggressive reorganizing of the seats and their body parts. Wes drove so that Gus could sit on Adam's lap, squeezed into one corner of the back seat, the trough sitting diagonally across most of the back seat and the front passenger seat.

Adam attempted not to feel one hundred years old as his knees were crunched to his chest. Gus was in her glory, rubbing at the trough and smelling her fingers, declaring that it smelled "fresh and dirty."

At the next estate sale they hit the Christmas lights

jackpot, thank god, because Adam didn't think he could spend much more time scrunched around the trough.

The house was prim and unappealing, with chintzy drapes swaddling every window and pastel wallpapers in every room. But it had clearly belonged to a family that celebrated Christmas with serious ceremony because an entire upstairs bedroom was packed with decorations. Everything from a faux gingerbread dollhouse to boxes of carefully packed collectible glass ornaments lined the walls.

Adam didn't care about any of that. He was perfectly happy with their ornaments made of pine cones and bits of ribbon and Gus' handprints in various sizes of salt dough over the years. But he snatched up the two paper bags of tangled lights and began plugging them in to see if any worked. A few didn't, but most did.

Gus' face lit up and Adam decided that actually, he could remain crunched in the car forever if it meant they found more lights and could make her vision come to life.

Wes had chosen to stay in the car, so while Gus poked at a train set, Adam quickly popped into the kitchen and opened the cabinets. There, at the bottom of a stack of Corningware, was a single Jeanette pie plate.

It was pumpkin pie, which Adam didn't have, and he held it to his chest gleefully.

"Found another one, Grandma," he whispered, feeling instantly embarrassed but not really caring.

His grandmother had been a source of warmth and caring in a childhood that severely lacked both, and Adam resolved once again that he would learn to make pie in her honor.

Riding high on their success, they decided to hit one more sale, but there were no lights to be found, and they headed home.

Back on Knockbridge Lane, they freed the trough from the car and wrestled it down the stairs to Wes' basement. Adam kept his eyes on Wes to ensure he didn't accidentally come face-to-face with Bettie or one of the snakes or god knew what else that Wes had crawling around in there.

"Can we please hang the lights now?" Gus asked, the required *please* doing little to temper her impatience.

Adam smiled and nodded and tamped down the squirmy feeling in his stomach that signaled his impending separation from Wes.

Chapter Eleven

Wes

Wes didn't want Adam to leave. It was a strange sensation for someone who generally craved solitude, but the evidence was right there, and Wes couldn't discount evidence.

So when Gus said, "Do you wanna help?" Wes said yes with the same speed as he'd accepted her invitation this morning. Of course, he hadn't realized when she'd offered treasure hunting that it would involve going to people's houses, which contained, well, people. He'd assumed they would be going to the woods or something. Still, he'd made it work by sticking to outbuildings and waiting in the car.

At this assent, he saw Adam's eyes widen but he thought it was simple surprise, not dislike. In fact, Adam moved a little closer to him.

Of course, that could simply have been his fear of spiders.

In Adam's driveway, they discovered that a few of the strands of lights they'd found at the estate sale were able to be linked together, so Gus decided those should run from one side of the house around the front door and over to the other side.

It gave the impression of a gingerbread house, door outlined in light.

Some of the other strands were so short that once plugged in they barely reached the roof. Wes suspected this would be a persistent issue with older lights, and lights clearly designed for indoor use.

There was a better way. A more organized way that would take advantage of the shape of the roof, and Wes began mapping out how they could balance out the splash of illumination on the side of the house where the outlet was.

Then he stopped himself. This wasn't an experiment. This was a little kid's vision, and he didn't want to ruin it.

Wes had never cared for Christmas. Growing up, it had been an excuse for his father to glad-hand and show off, and Wes had been one of the things on offer. As an adult, it became just one more occasion for large gatherings, small talk, idleness, and non-consensual touching.

But the joy on Gus' face as she watched the house become illuminated almost made Wes reconsider. He started to wonder if maybe, this Christmas, things might be different…

"I wanna go make inventions," Gus announced after they'd hung the final strand of lights and stood admiring their work.

She had told him in the barn that she planned to use her findings to "invent things." He had been impressed. It was how he had started himself, monkeying with bits and pieces of broken things, seeing how they might fit together. Seeing what they might create.

She reminded Wes of himself in a lot of ways: her intense interest in science and invention, her love of misunderstood creatures, her single-minded curiosity about the world.

In other ways, though, she was everything he'd never gotten the chance to be as a child: naive, trusting, friendly, carefree.

He admired more than he could say the fact that Gus could have her intense curiosities and never lose touch with people she cared about. That was Adam's doing, he imagined. Adam who seemed to care about everything.

"Do you know how to make pie?" Adam asked him as they went inside.

"I assume you don't mean of the 3.14159 variety?"

Adam bumped him with his shoulder and smiled. "No, I don't."

Adam began to wash the tall-sided plate he'd bought.

"My grandma used to have a whole set of these, and she'd make pies in them. See?"

He held it up to reveal a painted slice of pumpkin pie and a recipe painted on the plate. "I've never made a pie but it kinda seems like I'm supposed to since I found this, right?"

Wes wasn't a fatalist, so he didn't believe the two were related, but he knew what Adam meant: finding the plate was an encouragement to do something he wanted to do anyway.

"I can help, if you want?" he found himself offering.

Adam's whole face lit up, just as Gus' had when she looked at the illuminated house.

Wes placed this picture of Adam—sweet and excited and open—next to another picture in his head: one of Adam from the night before. Desperate and needy and so turned-on he could hardly breathe.

Both were gorgeous. Both were appealing. And together they made Wes' heart pound.

"What?"

"I said do you want to cut up this butter?"

Adam was peering at his phone and holding out two sticks of butter.

"This says it should stay very cold."

Wes stood next to Adam and looked at the recipe. He could feel the heat of Adam's body. He *knew* how perfectly they fit together and the temptation to pull Adam flush to his side was overwhelming.

"Do you have a food processor?" he asked, scanning the recipe.

"Huh? Oh. No." He squinted at the phone. "My grandma always did it with two forks."

"What if I make the filling and you make the crust," Wes offered, not wanting to tread on memories of Adam's grandmother.

"Great." Adam grinned at him.

"What kind of pie are we making?"

"Oh, right." Adam opened the refrigerator and the cabinets. "Apple, looks like. I don't have anything else. Do you know what to do?"

Wes didn't, but he had eaten apple pies before. How hard could it be?

"Sure."

He set about chunking the apples, mind drifting back to the night before. He'd floated home in a haze of pleasure, wonder, and—frankly—confusion. All these feelings for Adam were coming faster and more intensely than he'd ever experienced.

He'd wanted to know what Adam was doing, what he was thinking—make sure he was okay.

"I was watching you this morning," Wes blurted. "Through the upstairs window." And that had come out creepier than he'd intended.

Adam's blue eyes were curious, though.

"I was surprised you were awake," he said. "I thought you usually slept until afternoon."

"Usually. I couldn't sleep."

Their eyes were locked, and he saw Adam's pupils dilate.

"I can't sleep sometimes," Adam said.

"I know. I see the light come on downstairs. I see the flicker of the TV."

"I had insomnia in high school," Adam said. "It went away when I left town. I thought it was gone forever but it came back when Mason and I split up. Being alone, I guess?"

"What happened?"

Adam began smushing butter and flour together on the counter with two forks. It looked extremely unappetizing.

"I met Mason our last year of high school. He'd just moved here. He was cute and moody and smart, and I couldn't believe he was into me. I wasn't exactly popular in high school."

Wes bet high school Adam was a sweetheart.

"My parents...well, my father especially, was not good. We didn't get along. He's cruel and—" Adam broke off, shaking his head.

"Just, the opposite of what a dad should be. After high school, Mason was going to college in Boulder, so I went with him. It was great at first. He loved school and I loved not being anywhere near my parents. Or here."

Wes put the apple chunks in a bowl and poured sugar and cinnamon on them. That seemed to be what apple pie tasted like.

"One semester Mason took this photography class. He wasn't that interested in it, but I fell in love. At first I was just taking pictures of friends and random things I'd see around town. But then one of my friends asked me to shoot their wedding, and after that I started doing portraiture. It was awesome."

Adam looked lost in his memories, pie crust forgotten on the counter.

"River called me one day to tell me that our sister had had a baby. Hell, I didn't even know she was pregnant. River was just a kid. Marina tried with Gus for a little while, but she—"

He looked around to make sure Gus wasn't around, and lowered his voice.

"She loved Gus so much, but she never wanted to be a parent. Even if she had wanted to, she was working full-time to support herself and her boyfriend, and they couldn't afford any daycare. She said she'd rather die than let our parents have anything to do with Gus. So I...I offered to take her."

Adam blinked, remembering, and his face got the softest expression Wes had ever seen.

"I always wanted kids. Mason... Well, I should've discussed it with him first. I know that. I just thought... He was so great and Gus was so great, it *had* to work."

Wes cringed. "What happened?"

"He was furious. Said he was supposed to be focusing on finals, not on raising a kid. I told him I'd do all the work. I'd get up with her and feed her and change her diaper. I knew it was a lot to ask, but I thought maybe with a compromise..."

"You wanted her more than you wanted him."

Adam's eyes got wide. Had that been too harsh a phrasing?

"I guess...yeah. She was nonnegotiable. The thing is, when she started talking and walking around, Mason was more interested in her. He liked showing her off, liked playing with her sometimes. He wasn't a horrible father."

In comparison with Adam's own father, perhaps. And Wes'.

"But when she turned five, Mason started asking how long this was going to last. Like, like, like he thought we were gonna give her *back*. At first I figured he was just letting off steam. He'd started working at this tech company and he had really long days. He was tired, stressed, and of course having a kid doesn't exactly make it easy to come home at the end of the day and put your feet up.

"But we had a great babysitter who watched her while I was out on jobs, and she could've taken on more hours. It wasn't the hours, though. It turned out he just…wasn't willing to give anything up to be a father."

Adam started in on the butter mush again, wielding the forks like twin weapons.

"And Gus…there was Gus now. Gus was…she was everything. And I just knew. I was a dad now, and that was the most important thing. Maybe we could've found some kind of compromise eventually, I don't know. But I didn't want to compromise. I wanted a life with Gus.

"For the last year and a half or so we stayed living together but we weren't a couple anymore. We dated other people sometimes. Well, Mason did. I went on like three dates and all I could think the whole time was that I'd rather be hanging out with Gus or watching a movie. Or sitting quietly by myself not dealing with another person's ego. So that didn't go great."

"Did you tell Gus?"

"We didn't tell her while we were still living together. It was complicated enough without adding another variable. But it could only ever be a temporary situation. Eventually, something would change. And it did. Mason met someone he wanted to actually date. I thought…it would be hard for Gus, but we'd work it out. People do this all the time."

Adam trailed off and peered at the recipe on his

phone again. He sprinkled more flour onto the mush and started making it into a ball.

"I started looking for an apartment, but there was nowhere near Mason's place that I could afford working as a photographer. Not with any kind of money to pay for the help I'd need when Gus wasn't in school. Then it turned out, Mason didn't care if we stayed near him. Because he didn't want to be Gus' father anymore."

Adam's voice broke and Wes knew his grief was for Gus and not for himself. He took out a water glass and started rolling the ball of dough into a disk. When it tore, he smushed it together again. What he ended up with was a Frankenstein of ragged pieces of floury dough that he pressed into the pie plate.

"Should I put the filling in?" Wes asked.

"I think so?"

Wes poured the mixture of apples, sugar, and cinnamon into the crust and Adam put the other half of the pie crust on top of it, pinching the top and bottom together.

"My grandma used to do this cool, like, pinch and twist thing that made it look—nope, not like that. Oh, well."

He shrugged, put the pie into the oven, turned it on, and set a timer. They sat at the kitchen table.

"So you came here?"

"Yeah. Once it was clear Mason wasn't going to be part of our lives, it didn't make sense to stay. I just couldn't afford it. I was talking to River one day about six months ago. They were telling me all about how great the cat shelter was doing and how they had this whole group of queer friends now. How things were changing here. And they said they wished they could be a part of Gus' life. They were only a kid when she was born, so they'd hardly spent any time together. That clinched it.

"I felt horrible making Gus leave her friends, but coming here just made sense. Rent is affordable and River was excited to watch her sometimes. It seemed like a good solution."

"Could I see your pictures?"

"My photography?" Adam looked surprised. "Yeah, if you want."

"You said you loved it."

"Well, yeah."

Wes wanted to see what it looked like for Adam Mills to love something.

"Hang on a sec."

Adam returned with a beat-up laptop.

"This is some of my stuff."

The website was called *Adam Mills Photography* and its aesthetic was a combination of rustic mountain charm and elegance.

Adam scrolled through his portfolio and talked about the shots. He used words like *composition*, *balance*, and *focus*, but all Wes saw was how every single one of Adam's photographs looked happy.

Some were of people, and even those who weren't smiling had an air of lightness about them; of ease. The pictures of nature looked peaceful and joyous.

Even a shot of a general store at sunset managed to convey a sense of cheer.

"They're lovely," Wes said, then amended, "I don't know anything about photography. But they make me happy."

"Yeah?"

Adam's voice was soft and he was smiling.

"Yup."

Gus wandered into the kitchen then, hands and face smudged with gray streaks of grease.

Wes snorted to hide a laugh and watched Adam's eyes go wide.

"Daddy, can I have a snack?"

"Your timing is perfect," Adam said excitedly. "I just made apple pie."

"You did?"

Gus did not sound optimistic.

"Yeah. My grandmother used to make it in these special dishes, and I wanted to make it for you. That's your great-grandmother. You never met her…"

Adam kept talking while he scrubbed at Gus' hands and face. He asked her about what she invented, and she said it was a secret. Adam's eyes sparkled at Wes when she said that, and Wes got the idea that *secret* might be code for *nothing much*.

"Okay, sit down and get ready to have your mind blown with deliciousness!" Adam said.

Wes worried Adam might be overselling this a bit.

The timer went off just as Gus sat down and Adam grinned as if this were another sign of the fated perfection of this pie.

He opened the oven door and paused.

"Hmm. Um. Well? Hmm."

"Everything okay in there?"

"Oh, yeah. Well. I mean. Sure."

Wes and Gus exchanged a look and the second their eyes met, Gus raised an eyebrow conspiratorially and shook her head slowly, then put her hands to her throat and made a face like she was choking.

"Do you bake often?" Wes asked.

"Oh, sometimes," Adam said breezily. "I made cookies for Gus' class."

Gus made a crossed-eyes death face.

"And I always make her birthday cakes."

Gus shook her head rapidly in warning.

Adam turned to the table with the pie and Gus just smiled. When he turned away to get silverware, though, she caught Wes' eye again and shook her head deliberately, eyes wide.

A plate was placed before each of them, and Adam regarded the pie.

"Well, it doesn't look quite like what my grandma's used to look like. But I'm sure all pies are different?"

He cocked his head like perhaps looking at it aslant would change it from hideously misshapen to appetizing. After all, he had just spent ten minutes telling Wes about how changing perspective could change any photograph.

Adam shrugged. "Let's dig in!"

He cut into the pie and liquid bubbled up in the incision. With extensive wiggling, sawing, and scooping, he managed to excavate three pieces of watery pie.

Pieces was perhaps an overstatement. Globs? Piles.

Wes was not a picky eater. Food was just calories and calories were just energy and every human needed energy to get through the day. He took a bite of the pie.

It turned out *pie* was rather an overstatement as well.

"Mmm," Wes said, trying to swallow the bite very quickly to avoid tasting any more of it and also not swallow it because the filling was very hot and felt like it might scorch a path directly through his esophagus.

He blinked rapidly. His body's attempt to rid itself of this unholy abomination, or just a side effect of burning himself, he couldn't tell.

Gus was watching him, wide-eyed with shock, and he realized that she had been right to warn him off.

"Um," he gasped. "It's…"

Adam was watching him eagerly, fork poised over his own sluice of pie.

Gus was leaning back, arms crossed over her chest, looking at them like they were both fools.

Adam took a bite, and Wes saw the exact moment his hopes for a pie that was an homage to his beloved grandmother crumbled, unlike the gluey crust.

He looked horrified, lurched upright, and spat the pie into the sink.

He whisked Gus' plate away before she could touch it—though she'd clearly had no intention of so doing.

"Oh my god," he said. "I'm… I don't know what happened."

"You can't bake is what happened," Gus said, and Wes started to laugh.

It was so damn charming that Adam Mills, never having made a pie in his life, would decide that this pie would be perfection. It was so optimistic, so sweet, and so utterly unrealistic. But what the hell was reality anyway?

"It wasn't all his fault," Wes told Gus, to be fair. "I made the filling."

Gus shook her head slowly, looking worldlier than an eight-year-old had any business being.

"You should stick to your strengths," she told them both.

Chapter Twelve

Adam

It was three in the morning so of course, Adam was awake.

He rolled out of bed, sighing. This had been going on long enough that he knew there was no utility to lying there and trying to fall back asleep. It never worked, just left him irritable.

He'd been making his way through *Fanny and Alexander* the last few weeks, so he settled on the couch and cued it up to where he'd left off, three and a half hours in.

The movie was endless and beautiful and Adam let his mind wander along with the camera for a while.

The Christmas decorations in the 1907 Ekdahl house in *Fanny and Alexander* were grand and gorgeous—the kind of breathtaking drama that Gus must've hoped for when she said she wanted them to have the most Christmas lights ever.

eBay had provided a few more boxes of cheap lights, but Adam was quickly reaching the edge of the budget he could reasonably spend on this project and still have money left to get Gus anything for Christmas.

Biting his lip, he opened his Instagram again. There were a number of comments on his previous call to action—people saying they wished they could help, people offering to mail him lights, and people expressing how happy they were that he hadn't disappeared forever.

It had always given Adam a thrill to see the response to his photographs.

Maybe…

He paused Bergman and pulled on wool socks and a heavy sweater over his pajamas. After a quick peek to check that Gus was sleeping peacefully, he went outside, camera in hand.

He'd been minutes away from selling the camera before they moved. Gus was the one who stopped him, and now he was grateful she had.

Adam plugged in the lights and the house flared to life. Every other window was dark this late at night, so the lights blazed like fire in the night.

Adam backed down his driveway, considering his angles. At first, he shot it to make the lights look lush and luminous. Shot that way, it looked like an ordinary house with cheery Christmas lights—a well-composed shot, but still ordinary.

When he ditched the camera and shot with his phone from the other side, though, the image that emerged was of a bleak house and sparse lights that hardly stretched to cover it, all precariously plugged in to an overburdened power strip. It looked sad and pathetic.

It was unlike any other photo Adam had ever posted. But Adam wasn't a photographer anymore. He was just a single dad, working at a hardware store whose merchandise he knew nothing about, trying to make his daughter's Christmas wish come true.

Adam posted the picture.

Hello, everyone! he wrote in the caption. *I promised to show you my newest project, and...here it is. It's not my usual subject matter, but when your kid tells you that the one thing that would really make her happy for Christmas in a new town is to have "the most Christmas lights ever," well, what's a dad to do except try and make it happen?*

As you can see, it's not going so well -__- So here I am, asking for your help again. I would be so grateful if you wanted to help me make Gus' dream come true! You can mail any lights to me here, and I'll keep posting pics of our progress. My deepest thanks for anything you want to send, and I hope you're all having a happy December 1st!

"Adam?"

Adam wheeled around, clutching his chest, and dropped his phone.

Wes put his hands up. "Sorry, sorry, I didn't mean to scare you."

"Jesus. Hey."

Adam scooped up his phone, incredibly glad he'd put his camera down when he had, or it would've been in pieces.

"Sorry," Wes said again, looking sheepish. "I saw you from my basement window and I thought I'd… Anyway, hi."

He sketched a wave that was so awkward and geeky that Adam wanted to pull him into his arms and squeeze him tight.

Maybe it was residual daring from asking strangers for help on the internet after posting a *very* off-brand photo, or maybe it was the accumulated sleepless nights. Whatever it was, Adam followed his desire. He slowly stepped closer to Wes, giving him time to retreat, and when he didn't, he wrapped his arms around him.

They stood in the cold night air, before the blaze of lights. They held on to each other for a long time.

Adam breathed deeply, trying to figure out what Wes smelled like. It was something very green, like moss or wild grass, combined with something smoky, like…well, smoke.

Whatever it was, it clung to his sweater and Adam nuzzled closer, chasing it and Wes' warmth and running his hands up and down Wes' broad back.

"Hi," Adam said after a while. It was just an empty thing to say that meant *I'm here*, and Wes murmured back, "Hi."

Wes made no move to let go.

Was this happening? Were they doing this?

"Are we doing this?" Adam accidentally said out loud.

"Hugging in the middle of the night, in the middle

of the street, in the middle of the winter, when we both have perfectly good houses ten steps away? Yes."

"*One* of us has a perfectly good house," Adam retorted. "The other has a house of horrors, filled with spiders and snakes and bags of gas."

For a moment he thought he'd gone too far. Then Wes chuckled into his hair.

"Spiders and snakes need love too," Wes said placidly.

And Adam supposed that was true.

"The lights look…" Wes began, then cut himself off.

"Pathetic. I know. I was just trying to get some more."

Wes nodded.

"Can't sleep?" he asked softly, brushing Adam's hair back.

"Nope. I was watching *Fanny and Alexander.* I've been trying to get in the Christmas spirit for Gus' sake."

"What's *Fanny and Alexander*?"

"A really long movie by Ingmar Bergman about a Swedish family's Christmas in 1907."

Wes just blinked at him. "I guess that would probably help put anyone to sleep?"

"I like it," Adam clarified. "It's beautiful."

"Oh."

Wes looked nonplussed.

"You know, really long movies by Ingmar Bergman about Swedish families' Christmases in 1907 need love too," Adam said.

Wes grinned. "Fair."

"Do you want to come in?"

Wes darted a look back at his house where, Adam noticed for the first time, the basement windows glowed green.

"I was working," he said regretfully.

"Do you want to take a break?"

"A break."

Wes said it like it was as mysterious a thing as *Fanny and Alexander.*

"Cup of tea and a cookie?" Adam offered. "I didn't make the cookies, I swear."

Wes smiled.

"Okay."

Inside, Adam brought mint tea and gingersnaps into the living room. Wes was sitting on the couch looking pensive.

"When you said *this*, you did mean us, right?" Wes said before Adam even sat down.

"Huh? Oh, yeah. I meant…" Adam put the tea and cookies on the coffee table. "I mean, I like you. You're lovely. And hot. And smart."

And my kid worships you, he added silently. But that was way too much pressure.

Wes was watching and listening intently. Adam had never been the subject of such intense focus. He thought he could really get used to it.

"I just like you," Adam concluded simply.

"I like you too," Wes replied, still very intent.

Adam's heart stuttered.

"Cool," he said, mortifyingly.

Wes smiled. "Cool."

* * *

What Adam needed in his life was a best friend. Someone he could talk to about his burgeoning relationship. Someone to whom he could send texts like, Made out w W in middle of street. Are we boyfriends now?!?!?! And Dating yr neighbor who might be a vampire—Y/N???

Unfortunately, most of his friends had faded away when Gus entered the picture, and the rest had revealed themselves more Mason's friends than his when they split. He and River were close, but Adam wasn't sure if they were on romantic-talk terms quite yet.

So, lacking an actual best friend, Adam turned to what he did have: coworkers.

Bright and early Monday morning, Adam posed the question to Charlie and Marie.

"What would you think about dating your neighbor?"

He said it neutrally, casually, as if he didn't have his entire heart wrapped up in their answers.

Marie didn't talk much, but her facial expressions spoke volumes, and this one said beyond a shadow of a doubt *That is the worst idea I have ever heard and if you do that you will suffer.*

Or maybe he was just projecting.

Charlie was one of the fairest people Adam had ever met. He thought things through from all sides and he didn't jump to conclusions.

So when even Charlie hesitated, Adam felt his stomach fall.

"Yeah, okay," he said.

Hot tears pricked his eyes and he blinked them away and ducked behind the counter, pretending to pick up his pen.

Charlie turned away and pulled out his phone, and Adam considered the conversation over.

But a few minutes later, Rye, Charlie's partner, breezed through the door, dark hair flowing around his shoulders, kohl-rimmed gray eyes snapping.

"I received a bat signal?" he said.

Charlie cleared his throat.

"Oh," Rye said, and grinned. "I mean, oh, look, I've shown up here completely coincidentally and for no particular reason whatsoever."

Adam laughed.

Charlie shook his head and pulled Rye into his side with a fond expression. Rye patted his chest placatingly and smiled up at him.

"Tell us the whole story," Charlie said.

Adam blinked at him, overwhelmed by the generosity he was offering, and at work, no less.

For a moment, he couldn't speak for fear of crying again. Rye hummed absently and waved to an older man in the paint aisle.

"Keeping out of trouble, son?" the man asked.

"Never," Rye said with a grin. "You?"

"Naturally," he said, but winked at Rye with a twinkle that made Adam wonder.

"Okay, hit me," Rye told Adam.

Charlie swatted him playfully on the ass and Rye turned a wolfish look up at him, raising one eyebrow.

This. This was what Adam wanted. A partner. Someone he had rapport with. Someone he could joke around with, depend on, call and know he would show up.

"I'm falling for my neighbor and I'm scared it's gonna be a total disaster," Adam blurted, then clapped his hand over his mouth.

Falling for him? Oh, shit, I am *falling for him,* Adam thought.

"Back up," Charlie said.

Adam blew out a breath and told them the whole story.

"He's incredible," he said. "And Gus already worships him. And that's what I'm afraid of. What if things don't work out and she gets attached and then we're living right across from this man who she loved and now he doesn't want anything to do with her? I can't do that to her again. Not after Mason," he added under his breath.

Charlie and Rye were telegraphing over Adam's head, and even Marie's expression had softened. Less *Your choices will wreak ruin and misery* now, and more *Oh, you poor fool of love; I pity you and your daughter.*

"Ah, at the risk of overstepping," Charlie began, then seemed to reconsider, and didn't finish his sentence.

Rye rolled his eyes.

"You're not talking about Gus; you're talking about yourself," Rye asserted.

Adam froze.

"Yeah. I mean, it's true about Gus too. I get it. But this is definitely about you."

Marie gave the tiniest nod, and it was like a judgment from on high.

Adam looked to Charlie, who seemed like someone who'd never been afraid of anything.

Charlie said, "I know you're worried about your daughter. You'd never want to set her up to be hurt. But part of being a parent is trusting that you've raised a person who can handle negative emotions, not be drowned by them. And you'll be there to support her if she's upset. I agree, the real issue is you."

The Real Issue Is You: The Adam Mills Story.

Adam sighed, but wasn't Charlie right? Wasn't Gus already hurting from everything with Mason, and wasn't she dealing with it beautifully? He was helping her, and she was doing great. He was the one who couldn't sleep, had abandoned his passion, and was attempting to make pie.

Rye chimed in, "I don't know shit about kids, but I bet your daughter would want you to be happy, wouldn't she?"

Adam *knew* that was true. It was Gus, after all, who'd stopped him from selling his camera in Colorado; Gus who'd told him he loved taking pictures, so he had to keep it. It was Gus who, River had confided in Adam, had confided in River that she was worried Adam was sad because he'd left his friends behind.

His daughter was a sweet, empathetic person. She would absolutely want him to be happy.

Rye leaned in, expression mischievous.

"You're welcome. Also. Have you f—"

"Rye!" Charlie barked.

Rye grinned and shrugged. Then winked at Adam.

"Okay, but how was it, though?"

Adam let a slow, appreciative smile spread across his face.

Chapter Thirteen

Adam

"Daddy, don't be mad, but…"

Adam opened his eyes. Apparently he'd managed to sleep through the night, which was wonderful.

The beginning of that sentence, however…

He was instantly awake.

"Are you okay? What's wrong? What happened?"

"I'm fine," she said instantly. "It's just… It's Bettie…"

Panic struck Adam.

The night before, in the spirit of facing his fears, being bold, and living expansively, he had said yes when Gus asked him if Bettie could have a sleepover with her, even though the idea of the tarantula in the house horrified him.

He'd instructed Gus explicitly on being responsible with Wes' pet—and, fine, had taken Wes aside to say, "Are you absolutely, positively *sure* you want an eight-year-old in charge of Bettie?" in the hopes that he would see reason and change his mind.

He had not.

Adam had spent the last several days worrying about starting a relationship with Wes. But if Gus had hurt or killed Bettie, he could stop worrying about that, because Wes would probably want nothing more to do with them.

When he spoke, his voice was choked and high.

"What happened to Bettie?"

Gus' eyes went wide.

"Oh, nothing. She's fine."

Relief flooded Adam, and he closed his eyes.

"Good, good."

"It's just… I can't…exactly…find her."

"What!"

Adam jumped up, skin acrawl.

"I just took her out for a few minutes," Gus explained. "Wes *said* it was okay. And she was so sweet, crawling on my arm, and then I guess I must've fallen asleep for just a *minute*—"

"Okay, okay, okay," Adam said, trying to tamp down his horror and panic in front of Gus. "No problem, we'll just look for her. Okay."

But although his brain sent the message *Get off the bed and go look for the huge tarantula crawling around your house*, his body didn't seem able to carry it out.

"Daddy. Are you getting down?"

"Hmm? Ohmm, sure, yep."

Adam did not get down.

"Daddy?"

Adam nodded fervently, trying to figure out what to do.

"Uh, just hand me my phone, would you, sweetie?"

Gus did, and he dialed with shaking fingers. It was

morning, so he doubted Wes would be awake, but it was all he could think of to do.

A groggy-sounding Wes answered, and relief rushed through Adam.

"Wes, Wes, can you come over? Please!"

Wes was instantly alert. "Are you okay? Should I call someone?"

"No, no, I'm fine. I…it's…"

Gus took the phone from him.

"Hi, Wes. It's Gus. Can you help me look for Bettie? She's crawling around somewhere and Daddy's *too* scared. Okay, bye."

She tossed the phone on the bed and bounced cheerily out the door.

"I'll let him in," she called.

Adam did some deep breathing with his eyes closed, then realized that with his eyes closed, Bettie could crawl onto him and he'd never know. So he opened his eyes.

To find Wes standing in the doorway of his bedroom, looking at him with a strange expression. Amusement? Scorn?

No. Fondness.

Wes looked under the bed, in the closet, and all around the room, then came to the edge of the bed and held out his hand.

"I'm *so* sorry about all this," Adam said, taking his hand. *All this* encompassed approximately forty things at this point.

"It's okay," Wes said simply.

Adam let himself be soothed, and Wes tugged him into his arms, lifting him easily to the floor.

"I'll just make some coffee," Adam said. Coffee would make everything better.

Wes didn't let go of his hand but reeled him in and tipped his face up.

"Are you okay?" he asked.

"Um, it's honestly not the best wakeup call I've ever received, but I'll be fine. Once you find her," he added with a grimace and a little push.

Wes nodded, letting himself be pushed. Then he doubled back and caught Adam in a kiss.

Adam didn't have time to think about how he hadn't brushed his teeth yet or Gus could walk in at any moment. All he could do was be joyfully, gloriously kissed.

Thoroughly melted and in much better spirits, Adam made his way down to the kitchen, put the kettle on, and collapsed into a chair. It was only eight o'clock in the morning and already he was exhausted.

He got the box of pancake mix down from the cupboard—filed under *P* for pancake; god, Wes was so damn cute—put on the new Rhys Nykamp album, and lost himself in daydreams about more kisses from Wes as he made pancakes.

When he heard Gus' triumphant, "Bettie!" he felt a wash of relief.

"Pancakes!" he called, and Gus came galloping down the stairs, Wes following with a discreetly draped box under his arm that he placed near the front door before coming into the kitchen.

"Where was she?" Adam asked trepidatiously.

"The shower," Gus chirped gleefully, shoving pancakes into her mouth.

Adam pushed that image as far from his mind as possible, in the interest of ever cleaning himself again.

Wes sat down at the third plate Adam had set and took a sip of coffee.

"Don't worry," Gus told Wes with her mouth full. "They come from a mix."

Adam snorted. "I think what you meant to say was, 'Thank you for breakfast, and all the other meals you make for me so I don't starve to death.'"

Gus grinned. "Thank you for breakfast and all the other meals you make for me so I don't starve to death."

"That's what I thought."

Gus giggled.

"Gus and I are going to The Dirt Road Cat Shelter, where River works, to visit them and play with some cats. Wanna come with us?"

Adam said it casually, but he dearly wanted Wes to say yes. Of course, he had likely woken the man up just hours after he went to bed, and scared him into thinking his beloved pet was lost.

"I mean, I know cats aren't your animal of choice…" Adam gave him an easy out. "But no one will be there except River."

"I like cats," Wes corrected. "I just don't like them more than snakes and lizards."

"Yeah, come!" Gus said. "River showed me a video

of this cat they have there who always walks back-ward."

Wes' and Adam's eyes met, and Adam raised an eyebrow, and after a moment, Wes nodded.

"Okay."

"Yay!"

The Dirt Road Cat Shelter had begun its life as a house Rye Janssen inherited from a grandfather he'd never known. Over the course of the last two years, with a lot of help from River and many other residents of Garnet Run, Rye had built it into a first-rate shelter, with a huge social media following, adoption events, and, recently, a line of bespoke cat treats.

The outside of the shelter had retained the cabin shape, but the inside was nothing like one. The entrance was a set of two consecutive doors to keep cats from getting out, because inside, rather than being contained in pens, the cats had free rein of a complex network of cat ramps, tunnels, and obstacles that ran along the upper half of all the walls and led to a back room that was completely openwork metal mesh backed with Plexiglas that looked outside, so the cats had a panoramic view of the trees behind the shelter.

River grinned when they walked through the door, their blue eyes, usually wary, lit up with excitement.

"River!"

Gus ran at them and grabbed them around the waist, and River tweaked Gus' unruly ponytail.

"Hey, Bug. You wanna see some cats?"

"I wanna see the one that goes backward."

River smiled.

"Hey, Adam. Hi, Wes."

Adam hugged River and Wes shook their hand.

There was no one else in the shelter, so River led them to the room full of toys and beds where most of the cats spent their days. Many of them snoozed in puddles of sun. Others batted at toys, scratched the posts in the corners, and tumbled around with one another.

"This is Archimedes," River said, leading them to a large black cat with long whiskers and owlish yellow eyes.

Gus plopped down beside the cat and peered at it.

"Come here, Archimedes," River said, and threw a felt fish.

The cat scrambled toward the toy, but did so backward, with its head turned around to watch where it was going. When he got there, he tossed it himself and ran forward. Then got it and ran backward again.

"Whoa!" Gus exclaimed.

Wes leaned close to Adam.

"You really think that cat's cuter than Bettie?"

To be fair, the cat's movements had given Adam a bit of an *Exorcist* vibe, but he still thought it was adorable.

"Yes, because *cats*."

"It's just because certain animals are socially constructed as cute and others as scary," Wes grumbled.

Adam knew it was true. He made a silent promise to himself that he wouldn't say anything negative about Wes' pets again. Even if he was scared of them, it was no reason to rain on Wes' slimy parade.

River introduced them to some of the other cats and one of them took a liking to Wes. It was a small orange cat named Shirley and it kept pouncing Wes' legs whenever he walked past.

"You looking to adopt a cat by any chance?" River asked.

Wes scooped Shirley up and looked at her.

"I don't know if she'd get along with Janice and Banana."

"His raccoons," Gus explained to River.

River raised their eyebrows and nodded, the picture of diplomacy.

"Well, if you decide you want a cat, she definitely likes you."

"I'll think about it," Wes said. "Thanks."

He gave Shirley a pat on her little head and deposited her onto the nearest cat ramp.

Rye and Charlie walked through the front door, waving hello, and Adam had a sneaking suspicion that River might have texted Rye to tell him Wes was here. He narrowed his eyes at Rye, but Rye just winked.

"Hey, Adam," Charlie said. "And this must be Gus."

He held his hand out to Gus somberly, and she shook it just the same.

"You're Daddy's boss," she said, sizing him up. And his size was about thirteen times hers.

"That's right."

"You should be really nice to him because he's the best," Gus instructed Charlie very seriously.

"I will certainly try my hardest," Charlie pledged.

"This is Wes," Adam said, before his daughter could negotiate a raise or stock options on his behalf. "Wes, this is Charlie—he owns and runs Matheson's Hardware—and his partner, Rye, who created this place."

"Nice to meet you," Wes said. His voice sounded choked and he immediately retreated to the cat playroom. Gus and River followed, leaving Rye to grin at Adam and bump his shoulder, and Charlie to look on benevolently.

"That's him, huh?"

Adam nodded.

Rye opened his mouth to say something, but stopped and regarded Adam. At whatever he saw in Adam's face, he simply said, "Good for you."

Turning back onto Knockbridge Lane, Adam saw a pile of packages on the driveway. He spared a moment of irritation for the delivery person who hadn't put them on the front stoop, but it was quickly erased when he saw that there were more packages crowding the stoop.

"What the hell?"

Gus burst out of the car the second it stopped, and ran to the pile of boxes.

"Daddy, this one's for me!"

"Christmas presents?" Wes asked.

"Not from me," Adam said.

He had a brief swell of hope that maybe Mason had decided to shower Gus with gifts to make up for being an absolute failure, but he knew in his heart it wasn't the case. Mason wasn't the bother-with-the-post-office type any more than he was the amends-making type.

Adam insisted on opening one of the packages addressed to him first, in case this was a prank. He slit the first box open with his house keys and pulled out two boxes of Christmas lights.

"Oh!" Gus' mouth fell open.

"I'll be damned," Adam said. "The Instagram post worked."

Darren and Rose McKinnon, the Mills' next-door neighbors, picked that moment to come outside with their sons who were the same age as Gus—Dustin and Derek, or Donny and Derek, or Dennis and Dunstan; Adam could never remember.

Wes retreated to the side of the house.

"Looks like Santa came early this year, huh, sweetheart?" Darren McKinnon called to Gus.

"Oh, there's no such thing as Santa," Gus called back.

The McKinnons looked scandalized and Rose clapped her hands around either Derek or Dunstan's ears to try and shield them, but she was too late and had only the two hands.

"Of course there's a Santa Claus," she called, eagle eyes trained on Adam. It was clear she expected him to correct Gus. He smiled back at her, no intention whatsoever of doing so.

Gus laughed, then she waved. "Hi, Drake, hi, Dakota."

They ignored her.

Adam stopped bothering trying to remember their names.

Darren and Rose shepherded their kids to the car and drove off without another word.

"I don't think you're supposed to tell other kids that Santa doesn't exist, sweetie."

Gus shrugged.

"Santa's stupid. If Drake and Dakota want to think some old man is climbing down their chimney that's their problem."

Wes emerged from the shadows, nodding like this was a perfectly reasonable stance. Adam bit his fist to avoid laughing.

Having had the final word in the Santa Claus discussion, Gus turned to ripping open the rest of the boxes, eyes glowing with delight. All told, Adam's fans had sent him twenty-nine strands of lights: twenty-one white, five multicolored, and one package of three strands of bright pink lights, which Gus declared "Weird, but cool."

Many of the packages had notes with them, wishing Adam and Gus a happy Christmas and good luck with their project. A couple were from people Adam had worked with, and those had more personal messages.

One card was from a woman named Claire whom he'd shot a few years before, coincidentally on Gus' fourth birthday. During the shoot, he'd started crying thinking about how big she was getting and how much he loved her. He'd been mortified at his lack of professional veneer, but Claire had been lovely and hugged him, and told him that feeling never went away.

Her note was to Gus.

"Sweetie, this one's to you. It's from a friend of mine in Boulder. 'Dear Gus, I'm not surprised that your dad is doing something to make your dreams come true because that's the kind of father he is.'"

Wes put his arm around Adam's shoulders and squeezed.

When Gus had turned four, Adam had been overcome by the feeling of her growing up. The knowledge that his baby was gone and a small person was there in her place. Now, he looked at the strong, smart wiseass Gus had become, and his heart swelled with pride.

"'He loves you so much and I hope you never forget all the wonderful times you spend together. All my best, Claire.'"

"Thanks, Daddy," Gus said quietly, and fit herself to his other side.

With the man he was falling for on one side of him and the daughter he loved more than anything on the other side, Adam Mills felt utterly and completely at peace.

Chapter Fourteen

Wes

With the lights that Adam's Instagram followers had sent him, the Mills' house was beginning to look more like the competition for Most Lights Ever that Gus wanted.

Of course, they would never actually achieve that. Wes had looked it up the first time she mentioned it to find that the Guinness record for most Christmas lights ever on a residential property was held by the Gay family in Lagrangeville, New York, with 641,695 lights.

With each passing day, more and more lights were delivered. Adam had Wes take a picture of him and Gus standing in front of their newly illuminated house that he posted to his Instagram account, thanking everyone who had sent lights and announcing that they were still looking for more if anyone had them.

The Mills house was no Lagrangeville, but at least now when Gus got home from school and flipped the power switch, the lights no longer looked depressing.

In fact, this evening it looked downright inviting. The lights cast a glow around the house, every window downstairs was lit, and Wes imagined he could hear laughter and chatter coming from inside. He'd been glorying in the versatility of algae for hours now, but he couldn't help getting up every ten minutes or so, going to the periscope, and peeking at the Mills' house.

Don't do this, he cautioned himself. *Don't put yourself in this position. It won't end well.*

Sighing, Wes settled in front of his tub of algae once more, forced himself to stay seated, and tried to remember what his nice, private life was like before Adam and Gus had arrived on Knockbridge Lane, bringing with them the chaos that is a functioning heart.

"It's his sixtieth birthday," his sister said.

"I know."

"I'll pay for your flight," she went on. "Just come for Christmas."

"It's not about the money, Lana."

It had never, ever been about money, though his mother and sister refused to believe that.

"Then what?"

Wes could hear her begin to move around her house, doing other things. As always, his sister wasn't interested in any explanations other than her own.

"You know what. I can't spend time with Dad."

"You *won't* spend time with him. It's not like it'd kill you."

Also as always, Lana managed to say the exact thing that sent rage sizzling through him. She was the only one who made him feel this way. Even with his father, it wasn't rage. It was a gut full of guilt, pity, and a slow-burning resentment that would reach rage if allowed to kindle.

But Wes hadn't allowed it to kindle since he was fifteen. And he'd keep it tucked away inside him as long as he didn't have to spend time with his father.

Wes bit back the torrent of fury he wanted to unleash on Lana. It wouldn't do any good and would leave him with the bitter taste of guilt in his mouth for days to come.

"Yeah, you're right, Lana. It wouldn't kill me. I choose not to spend time with Dad. I'm hanging up now."

She didn't try to stop him. She never did. Because if he was the absent child, the child who didn't call on birthdays or come visit for holidays, who wasn't in publicity pictures with their father, who didn't send gifts, then she got to be the good child. The one who was there, who cared.

The one who had followed their father's plan for both of them, after Wes had torn it to pieces and flung it in his face.

Not that that had been his intention.

Wes jumped up and shook out his hands, needing to discharge all this energy. It wasn't late enough to go for a run yet—there might still be neighbors about—so he settled for doing pushups until his arms and back trembled and he couldn't hold himself up any longer.

He buzzed his hair as he did every week, turned

the shower as hot as he could stand it and ran a hand-ful of soap over his shorn hair. Once, that hair had been a feature people recognized. Wes made sure no one would ever recognize it again.

He walked around the rooms upstairs, air-drying, still irritated.

What would happen if he did go back to Los Ange-les? If he set the record straight in front of everyone.

He got as far as picking up his phone, when it rang in his hand.

Adam.

Just the sight of his name was like a cool breeze, dispelling the lingering heat.

"Hello?" he said, despite knowing it was Adam, the habit of learning to answer the phone that way unshakeable.

"Do you wanna come over and get drunk with me?"

Adam pitched his voice jovially, but it was clear he wasn't happy.

"Are you okay?"

"Yeah. I mean, I will be. Just a bad day." He sighed. "I've got boxed mac and cheese?" he offered, as if that was tempting.

"Okay."

"Yeah? Yay! Okay, come on over."

Wes stared at his reflection in the bathroom mir-ror after Adam disconnected the call.

It was the only mirror in the house, half fogged over from his shower.

Once, he had looked in every mirror he passed,

searching their reflections for what it was that made people care about his face. Whatever it was, he didn't see it. After things had imploded at home, an unexpected glimpse in the mirror was enough to fold him over with a clawing pain in his stomach.

He'd started training himself to look straight ahead so he didn't see himself in shop windows; to look at the water swirling down the drain so he didn't see himself in bathroom mirrors; to unfocus his eyes when speaking to people wearing mirrored sunglasses, so he didn't see his talking head in their reflection.

Dark eyebrows, intense blue eyes, a rather large nose, a mouth, a chin. Ears. Cheekbones. Stubble.

They were neutral in his mind. Clean of line, perhaps, and that seemed to be a thing people responded to aesthetically, but other than that…just features like any others.

Now, though, he found himself wondering what Adam thought of them. Might they appeal to Adam the way they once had to people he didn't care about?

Wes blinked and the man in the mirror blinked. Wes imagined it was Adam—beautiful, sweet Adam—looking back at him and he watched the man in the mirror's features become something hopeful, something tender, something yearning.

"Adam," Wes whispered, and the man in the mirror whispered it too.

Wes touched his lips to the lips in the mirror, wanting to see what Adam had seen when their lips met, but it was just a blur.

Scoffing at himself, Wes swiped at the mirror with the heel of his hand and went to get dressed.

Adam opened the door brandishing a bottle of gin and already-flushed cheeks. He smiled when he saw Wes and Wes felt as if he were the man in the mirror, looking out at the living, breathing world as if through a pane of glass.

Adam's expression dimmed at whatever he saw on Wes' face, and Wes saw exhaustion in the shadows beneath Adam's smiling eyes.

"What's wrong?" they said simultaneously.

"Jinx," Adam said, and gestured him inside.

Wes kicked off his boots and followed Adam into the kitchen.

"You like gin?" Adam asked.

"It's okay."

"You want some mac and cheese?"

"Okay."

"You wanna sit?"

"Okay."

"Have you recently been stricken with a curse that only allows you to say the word *okay*?"

Wes smiled.

"Okay," he teased, and Adam grinned.

"Oh, good. Then, uh, do you want to help me hang approximately one million strands of lights tomorrow that people have sent?"

"Okay," Wes said.

Adam rolled his eyes. "I was just joking."

"I know. But I'll help. You're a menace on the ladder. Can't have Gus orphaned, can we?"

He'd been going for levity but swore at himself internally when Adam's face fell.

"I'm sorry," Wes said instantly. *Not* the thing to say about a kid whose mother hadn't been able to care for her and whose other father had abandoned her. "I didn't mean…"

Adam shook his head.

"It's not that. I got home from work today and all Gus wanted to talk about was why Mason wasn't going to be with us for Christmas. And I don't want him here, but I'm so furious that he won't be here. For Gus, I mean. River told me she called him today while they were here and left a message on his voice mail and he never called back."

Wes felt his earlier anger flare back to life, only now it was directed at Adam's ex.

Adam put a bowl of macaroni and cheese in front of Wes. Clearly he'd been spending more time with Adam and Gus than he even knew, because the first bite of neon orange goo tasted familiar and homey.

"Here's to dad problems," Wes said, toasting Adam with another spoonful.

"Oh my god, *you* have a father?" Adam's blue eyes got comically large. "Tell me everything. I assumed you had sprung fully-formed from the head of Zeus or something, from the amount you talk about yourself."

"Nah, that's my sister, Athena."

Adam laughed, then said, "Wait, you don't really have a sister named Athena do you?"

"No. Lana."

"Okay, just checking."

Adam poured something into cups with the gin and handed one to Wes.

"Gin and mac and cheese. Parenthood classic."

"Cheese," Wes said, and clinked his bowl with Adam's.

Adam smiled but his brows wrinkled.

"You're in a weird mood. Or is this normal for you once you get comfortable with people?"

Wes tried to remember the last time he got comfortable with people. Only Zachary came to mind.

"Weird how?" Wes asked.

"Funny."

"I'm hilarious," Wes said seriously.

Adam smirked at him.

"It's cute you think I'm gonna be distracted from your dad problems."

Wes shoved more mac and cheese in his mouth and gave Adam an innocent look.

"Here, take this." Adam picked up the drinks and his bowl and gestured for Wes to bring his. "And come sit down."

They settled on the couch in the living room, farthest from Gus' room. Adam turned on the TV where a video of a wood fire played.

"Until I can have a real one," Adam said.

The fire crackled cozily, and Adam pulled a quilt over them. The first sip of the cocktail—make that *concoction*, Wes revised as the taste registered—cooled his lips and warmed his stomach. The second tasted slightly less weird.

"What is this?"

"Gin and apple juice. I don't make cocktails much anymore," he said sheepishly.

It wasn't precisely disgusting, so Wes knocked it back and chased it with the last bite of his mac and cheese. Then he took a deep breath and began to tell Adam Mills a story he hadn't told in fifteen years.

"My dad's an actor in LA. That's where I'm from. When I was little he landed a pretty good role on a soap. So he had steady work my whole childhood."

"Whoa, what soap?" Adam asked excitedly. "Sorry, never mind." He mimed locking his mouth and throwing away the key.

"When I was twelve, he decided it was time to make the leap to film. It was all he talked about."

Every night at dinner—when he was home for dinner—and every morning at breakfast, his father detailed each line of his resume that would make him appealing and unappealing. He monologued about his looks, his ability with different accents, his charisma.

Lana, three years younger than Wes, hung on their father's every word. But Wes' mind would wander. He thought about the way the tree at the corner of their street grew at an odd angle. He thought about the lizard he'd seen snoozing in the sun on their deck. He thought about the way the air smelled electric before a storm.

"Was he good?" Adam asked.

"He was okay, I think. Good enough for soaps, but nothing special."

And that was the part that had really killed his father. He yearned for the kind of acclaim that came from uniqueness, never satisfied to be part of an ensemble. He wanted to be a star.

"I don't exactly know how it all went down. But around that time, my dad started telling me there was a role for me on the soap. I wasn't interested and I told him so. He thought I was just playing it cool, but I really had no interest. It sounded so boring. Standing around all day, waiting for your scene to come, and then saying some fake words? What was appealing about it?"

Adam smiled and took his hand, tracing his palm under the blanket with warm fingers.

"You would think that." He said it fondly.

"When I told him I really, truly had no interest, he told me that he'd made a deal with his agent to get me as her client. She wanted me. I don't know why. But the way my dad put it to me was that either I did the show and he got to be a movie star, or I said no and flushed his dreams down the toilet."

"That's horrible," Adam murmured, squeezing his hand.

"Yeah. Now I know it was nonsense. My dad probably wanted the publicity that would come from having a father and son both in the business. Something like that. But at the time, I honestly thought if I didn't do it I'd be wrecking my dad's career."

"Lemme guess. You did it?"

Wes nodded.

"When I told my dad I would do it…it's…"

The look on his father's face had been—he realized now—relief. But at the time, he'd thought it was joy. Joy that Wes was causing. And it was the first time he felt like his dad was glad to have him around.

"Usually he just thought I was weird. He never understood my interest in science or why I wanted to take things apart and learn how they worked. He wanted me to be interested in Hollywood and publicity. Or at least sports. Something he could talk to me about. Something I could discuss at parties. So when I said I would do it, it was like I finally did something he could understand. Something he approved of."

That night at dinner, Wes' dad spoke about work as if it included Wes; as if they were embarking on a journey together. It felt good.

Six months later, when Wes started rehearsing, his father walked him onto the set with a hand on his shoulder, proud to show him off to everyone.

This is my son, he'd say with a wink. *He'll be playing Crawford Magnusson*. People on set thought that was just precious: Wes playing his real father's son on the show.

"It was supposed to just be a short subplot," Wes explained. "My character showed up and revealed that my dad had a son he never knew about. Then I was supposed to die in a bank robbery. But when it started airing, something weird happened."

Adam frowned and squeezed his hand harder.

"They didn't want to kill my character off anymore. They kept writing more scenes for him."

"You must've been really good," Adam said.

Wes shook his head.

"My character was a slimeball. I don't know. But my dad got weird. Weirder. He talked about how great it was. What a success to have a role expanded. But he was clearly upset."

"Jealous," Adam murmured.

"Maybe."

"Did you stay on the show?"

Wes bit his lip, afraid Adam would respond the way his family and friends had at the time. The way his father told him every normal person would respond: with scorn at his ingratitude.

"The thing is…" Wes noticed he was rubbing his shaved head over and over with the hand not holding Adam's, and he forced himself to stop. "People started to look at me. To *notice* me."

Nausea crept through Wes' stomach and burned in his throat.

"They would talk to me. Yell at me from across the street. *Touch* me. The first time it happened I tried to do what I'd seen my dad do. I smiled and said hi. But I didn't know what they wanted. After a little while I… just needed to get away. I was with my dad, going into the studio, and a girl tried to cut a piece of my hair."

The nausea swelled and Wes regretted every bite of macaroni and cheese.

"I freaked out," Wes made himself say. "It wasn't about my hair. Not really. It was… I hated the attention. I hated people seeing me. People paying attention to what I ordered in a cafe or what shirt I chose to wear."

Adam's eyes were wide. "That sounds horrible."

Wes nodded. Something had happened to him, then. Something confusing and insidious. The more visible he became on the outside, the more he became invisible to himself. Every worry about being seen, every thought spent on the perceptions of those who might see him, stripped away the part of himself that engaged with the world on his own terms. That wondered what would happen if he put the coffee machine together backward, or how a plant could grow through concrete.

The inner peace he'd always possessed when tinkering, experimenting, observing, had been obliterated by the threat of constant observation.

Wes couldn't stand it. Without his questions, without his experimentation, he didn't know who he was. And worse, he didn't care.

"I quit. I told my dad I wouldn't do it anymore. It didn't go over well. My dad told me I was making a huge mistake. That I was an idiot to throw away something that anyone would kill for."

"But *you* wouldn't," Adam said fiercely. "You didn't want it."

Wes shook his head.

He would never forget the look in his father's eyes when he'd told him. A furious disgust that had burned as hot as his approval had when Wes agreed to do the show.

You'll change your mind, his father had said at first. *Sleep on it. I know, fame can be a lot of pressure.* Adam had slept on it, knowing his mind was made up, and the next morning he'd tried again. The

mild mentor was gone, then, and his father's judgment had rained down—falling like acid rain on their
tenuous connection until it was eaten away to nothing but holes.

"I was foolish to think I could just walk away and
it would be over," Wes said. "The publicity machine
runs on speculation, and my privacy was the chaff
that got spit out in the process."

Where In the World is Crawford Magnusson?!,
Soap Digest had asked on its front cover as Wes tried
to go to school, go to the store, hang out with his
friends. People seemed to recognize him more than
ever. They would bombard him with questions about
when he was returning to the show.

After a group of tourists surrounded him when
he was coming out of a bookstore, Wes shut himself
in his bedroom, staring at himself in the mirror. His
hair had been shoulder-length, then. A fall of shiny,
tight curls that bounced as he walked. It was distinc-
tive. Noticeable.

Wes shaved his head with his father's electric razor
and dumped his curls in the garbage can. He'd kept
his head shaved ever since. It had worked, mostly.
Little by little, the longer he stayed out of the spotlight, the public lost interest. Eventually, they left
him alone.

And so, it turned out, did his father.

For the year after Wes quit, his father hounded him,
guilted him, berated him for his choice and his selfish-
ness. But when it became clear Wes would not return,
his father was simply done with him. Wes served no

purpose for his career, so Wes was of no interest any longer. He only had one thing to say, and he'd said it with utter conviction: "You will regret this."

Then Lana turned thirteen and told their father that she wanted to be an actor, and a new alliance was made.

"So what's the deal now? Do you have a relationship with your dad?"

"I text him on his birthday. Sometimes he responds."

Thank you with a period at the end was usually the response, when there was one. Once, a few years ago, the text had come through late at night. Wes had been up, as was his habit, but his father was clearly drunk and alone, likely on the couch in Wes' childhood home, staring at the picture of himself that hung over the television: standing on the red carpet in a tux and shiny shoes, young and vibrant, laughing at something just out of frame.

We really could've been something, son, that text had said. It all could've been different.

Wes hadn't responded.

"My sister called earlier. My dad's birthday is right before Christmas. She wanted me to come home. It's his sixtieth."

"Are you gonna go?"

"Hell no. Lana doesn't actually want me to come. She just wants to be able to tell my parents she tried to get me to."

"Do you get along with your sister?"

Wes could remember her as she used to be, when

she'd sit quietly in the corner as he tinkered, knowing she'd get kicked out if she made a sound but wanting to be near him.

"We never had much in common, but we got along fine. She went into acting after I quit. My dad helped her get started."

Adam was silent for a moment, then looked up with narrowed eyes.

"I'm sorry, I *have* to know who your dad and sister are. I'm too curious."

Wes chuckled. He'd heard Gus say that too: *I'm too curious*.

Wes pulled out his phone and showed Adam their IMDb pages.

"You changed your name?" Adam asked.

"It's my mom's last name."

"I don't think I've seen anything they're in, but they definitely look familiar." He made a picture of them at the Emmys bigger and brought the phone closer.

"You look a bit like your dad, I guess. But not like your sister."

Wes nodded. Adam's finger hovered over the screen.

"You can look," Wes said, resigned.

"Huh?" Adam looked at him innocently.

"Go ahead, it's fine."

Adam bit his lip, then clicked the link on his dad's profile that led to Westley Brennan.

Wes gazed at the flickering fire on Adam's television.

"Oh my god, your hair," Adam murmured. "Wow."

Then he passed Wes back the phone. "You were pretty cute," he said.

Then he swung over Wes' lap and put his hands on Wes' shoulders.

"But you're absolutely stunning now."

Wes shrugged. He knew Adam meant well, but he still didn't like to have his looks commented on.

"I won't say it again if you don't want," Adam said, perceptive as ever. "There's so many more important things about you that are also stunning."

Wes' heart fluttered.

"Yeah?" he asked, and heard the roughness in his voice. He couldn't quite bring himself to ask what they were, but he desperately wanted Adam to tell him.

"Oh, yeah."

Wes swallowed hard. Adam's blue eyes were luminous and tender.

"You're very kind," Adam said.

Wes closed his eyes. His family would certainly disagree with that. A soft kiss was dropped on one eyelid, then the other.

"You're incredibly smart."

A kiss on each cheek.

"You're kinda funny, turns out."

Wes snorted and got a kiss on his forehead.

"You're generous."

A kiss on his chin.

"And you're very, very sexy."

Adam caught his mouth in a sweet kiss that deepened into searching tongues and the hot crush of lips.

Wes' body came alive with desire for the sweet, sexy man in his lap.

"Adam," he breathed between kisses.

"Wes, god. I like you so much," Adam said.

Heat bloomed in Wes' stomach. Not the heady fever of lust but the steady, banked heat of care. Of something you want to keep burning.

"I like you too," Wes said. Then added, "So much," because it paled in comparison to what he felt.

The expression of joy on Adam's face was something Wes would carry with him for a long time. Adam's fingertips traced his face.

"I was thinking of you. Earlier," Wes continued, the confessions seeming to spill out of him tonight. "I couldn't concentrate. Kept wondering what you and Gus were doing. How you were."

He brushed Adam's blond hair back from his face, the fine strands catching on his roughened palms.

"I was thinking about you too," Adam said with a giddy smile. "I didn't want to bug you."

"I like bugs," Wes murmured, and Adam giggled, then shushed him with a kiss.

Adam ground his hips against Wes' thickening erection and Wes threw his head back.

"C'mon," Adam said, standing and tugging at his hand. His eyes were heavy lidded, lips swollen. He was irresistible.

Wes allowed himself to be led down the hall to Adam's bedroom, but the second the door was locked behind them, he grabbed Adam and threw him onto the bed.

Adam moaned, looking up at Wes and biting his lip. *Yes*, he mouthed.

Wes stripped him and pressed his shoulders to the mattress, licking at his pert nipples. Adam writhed beneath him, trembling at each swipe of Wes' tongue and gasping at each nibble of his teeth.

Adam fumbled in the bedside table, coming up with a bottle of lube and a condom and dropping them on the bed. His pupils were blown.

"Want you," he said. "Please?"

Soles of his feet on the bed, Adam let his knees fall apart, baring creamy thighs, dark blond hair, and a ruddy erection already leaking for Wes.

"Damn." The scent of skin and desire was heady.

Wes bent to kiss the pale skin of Adam's inner thighs. He rubbed his cheek on the soft flesh and Adam gasped. Wes rubbed harder, and the skin turned pink. Adam's hands fisted the sheets.

"What else do you have in there?" Wes murmured, eyeing the drawer that had produced lube and condoms.

Adam flushed, but grinned. He twisted just enough to pull open the drawer, and Wes was treated to a colorful glimpse of toys. Adam pulled out a small black toy that fit over two fingers. He pressed a button and it began to vibrate.

Adam raised an eyebrow and moved to put it away and grab something else, but Wes stopped him.

"Show me the rest later," he said, and took the small vibrating ring.

Wes undressed slowly, watching Adam's flush

move down to his neck, then his chest. He was so pale Wes could trace the veins from his throat to his groin.

"God you're gorgeous," Adam groaned as Wes bared himself. Then he clapped a hand over his mouth. "Sorry. Said I wouldn't mention your looks."

Wes was moved.

"It's okay. Feels different in this context. Thanks, I mean," he added when his brain caught up to him. "You're beautiful, Adam. Truly."

Adam smiled and drew him down for a kiss. Their erections caught and Wes pressed them together, groaning at the contact.

They rocked together as they kissed, and Wes let the heat grow between them. He could feel Adam leaking against his hip and drew back to put the condom on.

Adam handed him the lube, and Wes coated two fingers. He lifted Adam's hips.

"Okay?" he murmured, pressing gently inside.

Adam groaned and nodded quickly.

Wes slid his fingers deeper into the inferno of Adam's body. There was the initial resistance, then it gave way, and he was a part of Adam. Part of his silky, clenching heat.

"Oh, god," Adam moaned. "Yes, yes, yes, that's so good."

Wes kissed his belly and found his prostate, rubbing it with the pads of his fingers.

Adam's eyes rolled back in his head and he went stiff. Then, when Wes rubbed harder, he let out a groan and melted around Wes' questing fingers.

"Oh my god that feels so good, unnghh."

Wes fingered him slowly, made sure his body was relaxed, then slid his fingers out, treasuring Adam's disappointed gasp.

He stroked lube onto his erection quickly, suddenly desperate to be buried deep inside his lover.

"Adam," Wes whispered. "I want you."

"Yes, please," Adam moaned.

Wes pressed the tip of his erection into Adam, relishing the slick heat. He made himself go as slowly as he could, gritting his teeth with restraint. But Adam gasped, grabbed at his shoulders, and pulled him closer.

Liquid heat shot up Wes' spine as he felt himself slide deep inside Adam. He was rocked by wave after wave of pleasure, and it took every ounce of restraint he possessed to pause and wait until Adam's body relaxed.

"Oh my god, Wes," Adam groaned after a few moments. "Yes."

Wes nodded, unable to summon a single word. He kissed Adam instead, put Adam's feet on his shoulders, and began to move inside him.

He angled his hips so his strokes would caress Adam's prostate and Adam opened his mouth in a silent scream.

Wes felt himself coming unspooled. The heat of Adam's flushed cheeks, the tender flesh of his thighs, the silk of his rose petal lips, and the hot clench of his body were so potent that Wes heard the groans spilling from his lips and felt his stomach tighten with lust.

Adam was moaning and clutching at him, the flush pinking his cheeks obscenely.

Wes slid the vibrating toy onto his fingers and flicked the tiny button to turn on the vibrations.

Adam's eyes got wide. Then one corner of his mouth lifted in a lusty smile and he nodded.

God, he was perfect.

Wes slid the vibrating toy over the tip of Adam's erection and felt every muscle in his body clench.

Adam swore and panted and Wes felt peace descend over him that he usually only felt in the lab. But here, all he wanted was to make Adam feel better than he had ever felt in his life.

"Oh god, oh god, ohgod, ohgod, ohgodohgodohgod," Adam chanted, coherence losing out to his body's needs.

"Yes, baby," Wes purred.

He thrust faster, seeking an explosion of the pleasure that mounted higher and higher. As he drove deeper inside Adam, he kept the vibrator tight to the ultrasensitive tip of his erection. Adam keened, throwing his head back.

"Wes, Wes, Wes, Wessss."

Adam's mouth fell open and every muscle clenched. Then he was gone, shuddering around a silent scream.

It was the hottest thing Wes had ever seen. Adam was spread out before him, writhing in ecstasy, and it was the last straw. Wes drove deep inside Adam and felt the burning pressure erupt out of him in wave after wave of perfect pleasure.

He shuddered with the intensity of it as he came down. Then Adam clenched around him and tendrils of pleasure grabbed him again, sending aftershocks juddering through him.

"Jesus Christ," Wes groaned, and collapsed on top of Adam. He buried his face in Adam's throat, breathing in the scent of his skin, glazed with clean sweat.

"Oh my god," Adam said, letting a hand fall heavily on Wes' back. "What the hell did you just do to me."

But it wasn't a question, and Wes hummed. The vibrator, buried in the covers now, buzzed its agreement, and Wes fumbled for it and turned it off.

"C'mere," Adam murmured. Wes slowly slid out of Adam and they both hissed with the loss. Wes took care of the condom then settled in next to Adam, gathering him in his arms.

"That was…outrageous," Adam said, and kissed his shoulder before snuggling closer. "In a great way," he clarified, and Wes chuckled.

He loved the weight of Adam against his chest and side, loved the feel of him wiggling closer under the covers, loved the scent of their combined pleasure lingering heavily in the air, and the sound of Adam murmuring sweet, sleepy things against his skin.

"I agree," Wes said, and Adam gave him a squeeze.

"Will you stay?" he asked.

He wanted to. He wanted to kiss Adam back to slumber if he couldn't sleep, and wake up to him, heavy and soft in the morning light.

"Is it okay? With Gus, I mean?"

"Mmm-hmm."

"Okay."

"Yay," Adam said happily, and cuddled closer.

Wes usually didn't go to bed for hours yet, so he knew he wouldn't fall asleep. But it didn't matter. If he got to hold Adam then he was exactly where he wanted to be.

Chapter Fifteen

Adam

Adam surfaced from sleep slowly, gradually becoming aware that he was held in strong arms and that a warm, muscular form was behind him.

Wes.

Adam felt his entire body flush with heat as memories from the night before came flooding back. It had been the best sex of his life. Wes had felt perfect inside him, gloriously nailing his prostate on every stroke. When he'd added the stimulation of the vibrator Adam had been done for.

And he couldn't wait to do it all over again.

Wes made a sleepy sound behind him and pressed his face into the crook of Adam's neck. It made Adam's stomach go gooey.

"Morning," Adam said softly.

"Mmng," was the sleepy response into his hair, and Wes' arm gathered him closer.

"You can keep sleeping," Adam said, "but I should—"

But he didn't get any further than that because that was the moment that Gus opened the door.

Only the door was locked, so she just banged on it.

"Daddy!" she said in a singsong voice far too peppy for early on a Saturday morning. "Daddy, I'm awake now!"

"Yeah, I can hear that, sweetheart. Why don't you go watch TV for a few minutes and I'll meet you in the living room."

"'Kay. Can I get juice?"

"Yeah."

Wes had buried his head under the pillow when Gus had started yelling, whether out of embarrassment or simply to muffle the skull-rattling noise Adam wasn't sure.

"Um. You okay under there?"

"Mmm-hmm."

"You sure?"

Adam pushed the pillow aside and Wes' arms came up and grabbed him, pulling him down on top of Wes.

Adam couldn't help the small *yeep* that squeaked out of him. He kissed Wes, and Wes kissed back, squeezing him tight.

It felt like home.

"So, do you want me to climb out the window and down the drainpipe or what?" Wes asked.

Adam's stomach fell.

"Oh. I...if you want."

"I don't think anyone ever really *wants* to climb down a drainpipe," Wes said.

But Adam wasn't in the mood to joke. He wanted to walk out of his bedroom with Wes as if it were normal. To make coffee and eat waffles with Gus, and...

What? Be a family?

The words were said in a nasty voice in his head, and it wasn't his voice. It was Mason's.

But Adam had let Mason ruin enough of his days when they were together; he'd be goddamned if he'd let him do it now that they were over.

"Yes, actually," he told Mason's sneering voice in his head.

"Oh," Wes said. "Well, I was kind of kidding, but if you really want me to..."

"Huh?"

"Climb out the window."

"No, no. Oh. No, I don't want that."

Wes lay in his bed, gloriously naked, blankets pooled around his waist. With his shaved hair, he didn't even look morning mussed. He just looked like Wes all the time.

Adam wanted to see Wes in every conceivable scenario: getting out of the shower, covered in sweat, sleepy, grouchy, stuffing his face with spaghetti. He wanted to *know* Wes. He wanted to be with Wes.

"Aw, hell," Adam muttered. He'd been trying to cut the f-word out of his vocabulary so he didn't say it around Gus and it had resulted in some awkward phrasing.

"Hey," Wes said. "You wanna fill me in? I really will sneak out if you want. Although..." He eyed the window seriously, and Adam could practically see the calculations he was doing. "I don't think the drain-pipe will actually hold my weight."

He was making light of things. Giving Adam a

chance to collect himself. And it filled Adam with a fizzy sense of possibility.

Slowly, Adam leaned in and kissed Wes. His breath was a little sour and his lips were soft, and Adam kissed him again.

"Do you wanna come have some breakfast?"

"You sure?"

Adam nodded. "If you're okay with Gus making some assumptions."

"Would her assumptions be, um, correct?"

Wes' blue eyes were warm and searching, and Adam saw something vulnerable and nervous in them.

He cupped Wes' face, thinking about young Wes who'd experienced love as conditional. Whose family hadn't cared about his desires. Hadn't accepted him for who he was but only for how they could use him.

"If her assumptions are that we're dating," Adam said, "then I'd be okay with that being correct." He bit his lip. "Would you?"

Wes' smile was soft and peaceful.

"Yeah, I could deal with that hypothesis panning out."

"Such a nerd." Adam kissed him again.

"Such a romantic," Wes said, returning the kiss.

They dressed and went to find Gus. Just before they descended the final step into the living room, Adam grabbed Wes' hand. His heart felt like a hummingbird's in his chest, suddenly, at the thought of his daughter not approving of him and Wes.

Gus was lying on the couch, her head hanging over

the side, watching TV upside down. She claimed it was more interesting that way.

She smiled when she saw them, and then her eyes tracked down (well, up, for Gus) to their joined hands and her eyes went wide. Her mouth opened in a perfect O and she flipped right side up.

She bounced on the couch and clapped a hand over her mouth, something Adam had taught her to do when she had something she was about to say but wasn't sure if it was appropriate.

"It's okay, sweetie," Adam said.

"You! Are you? You're!" She bounced with each word.

"We're dating," Adam said.

He walked over to the couch and Gus stopped bouncing. Standing on the cushions she was almost as tall as him. Her expression was serious as she said to Adam what he'd said to her many times: "You made a *very* smart choice."

Adam burst into laughter that turned, in an instant, to tears. He grabbed Gus in a hug and squeezed her tight. Before becoming a parent he never could have imagined the singularly exquisite feeling of his daughter being proud of him. He cried happy tears into her messy blond hair.

"Thanks, sweetie," he gulped.

"Are you okay?" Wes looked concerned.

"He's fine," Gus said, unconcernedly patting Adam's head. "Daddy gets very emotional sometimes."

Her nonjudgmental explanation just made Adam cry harder.

He felt Wes' strong arms come around them both, holding them tight.

When Adam's tears dried and Gus got bored of hugging, they went to the kitchen and Adam put waffles in the toaster as Wes made coffee. Gus set the table and began a long, enthusiastically detailed description of the book she was reading about a girl who discovers alien life on Mars.

"Mars is not the most likely planet to play host to life forms," Wes said seriously.

"It's fiction," Adam said.

"Still!"

And Wes began an equally long and enthusiastically detailed explanation of the meteorological and chemical environment of Mars as compared with other planets.

Adam tuned them both out and watched as if it were a movie. He felt so utterly joyful—so full up with warmth and happiness—that it seemed his skin could hardly contain it.

"Be right back," he murmured, though Gus and Wes were too focused on aliens to notice.

In the bathroom, Adam stared at himself. His eyes looked shockingly blue against the redness left over from crying, and that almost got him started again. He'd always cried easily, but sometimes the tears felt so close to the surface that they just welled over.

He looked in the mirror and let his chin wobble and his lips tremble and his eyes fill with tears. He smiled at himself and said firmly, "It's brave to take risks. It's okay if things don't work out. It's still worth trying. Love is always worth trying for."

Love, love, love.

It was what he'd never felt from his parents. It was what he'd wanted so desperately with Mason, and realized wasn't there. He'd learned what love was from Gus, and now that he knew, he would never accept anything less.

"It's not silly to want love. It's not foolish to admit you want it."

"Daddy?"

Gus' voice came from the other side of the door.

"Be out in a sec, sweetie."

"Is your tummy not feeling good?"

Adam grinned.

"Nope, I'm fine. Be out in a minute."

"Okay."

Just when he thought she'd surely left, she said. "I ate your waffle."

Adam laughed, hand over his mouth. At his silence, Gus said, "I can make you another one."

"That'd be nice. Get Wes' help if it's still hot, though."

He heard her walk away and sank down on the toilet seat, scrubbing the tears off his face.

His daughter was a goddamned jewel. The amazing man he was quickly falling for liked him back. It was almost Christmas, his favorite time of the year.

Nothing could ruin Adam's perfect happiness.

Chapter Sixteen

Wes

Wes was on fire. He hadn't felt this alive since he walked into the lab his first semester at Caltech and saw the equipment that would enable him to carry out all the experiments he had in his head.

It was the buzz and pop of possibility, the tingle of potential.

It was happiness. He'd just never had a name for it before.

Telling Adam about his family, his past—putting it into words for the first time in years—had clarified it for him. His father had been wrong. Wes hadn't realized how muddy he'd allowed that to get in his mind after all this time. How much the guilt of choosing not to have a relationship with the man had complicated the story.

Now, though, eating waffles at Adam and Gus' kitchen table, seeing how everything Adam did was in service of showing Gus fairness, exposing her to honesty, both in fact and feeling, and giving her space to be herself, it was very, very clear. His parents hadn't been like that. They hadn't been like that at all.

"Hey, what's up?" Adam asked.

"Huh? Nothing. Just thinking."

"Anything good?" Adam said lightly, with a soft smile that said they could talk about it later if he wanted.

"You're an exceptional parent," Wes said. "That's all."

Adam's eyes went wide, then filled with tears.

Gus patted Adam's hand, then shoved another bite of waffle in her mouth.

"Thank you," Adam said thickly. "I...wow, thank you."

"What are we doing today?" Gus asked.

"Well, I thought we could hang some more lights. Wes said he could help."

"Can I climb the ladder?" Gus hedged.

"A little bit," Adam said. "And I get to stand right underneath you in case you fall."

Gus rolled her eyes but agreed, and it gave Wes an idea.

"Do you like the woods?" he asked Gus.

She nodded excitedly.

"Maybe after we hang lights we could go on a little adventure."

Gus immediately turned to Adam. "Can we?"

"What does *little* mean in this instance? Also *adventure*?"

Wes laughed.

"Just a little hike. In the woods. To a clearing that I want to check out."

"That doesn't sound at all like you're going to murder us," Adam mumbled. "Okay, sure. Lights, then being led to a mysterious spot in the woods."

"Yay!" Gus said, then ran to get dressed.

"I'm gonna run home and change," Wes said. "Feed the animals. Meet you back here in an hour or so?"

"Okay." Adam was gazing at him. "Can I have a kiss before you go?" he asked tentatively.

Wes didn't want him to ever feel tentative about asking for that. He stood and drew Adam into his arms. When their lips met, everything else melted away, and it was just them and this moment. Wes cupped Adam's cheek and kissed him again, light and sweet. Adam's eyelashes fluttered.

"Okay, bye," Wes said.

Adam smiled and gave a little wave.

When Wes closed the front door behind him, he felt a little tug in the region of his heart, as if with each step he took away from Adam he was leaving behind something essential.

It had only been twelve hours, but his own house felt dark and oppressive after being in Adam's cozy, airy home.

He made the rounds, feeding everyone, cleaning up, kissing lizard heads, scratching raccoon backs, and letting snakes slither their way around his neck.

After a shower and a change of clothes, Wes texted Zachary.

I really like him. Then, as he pulled on his shoes, I don't want to screw it up.

Good plan, Zachary texted back. I wish I had some advice, but I've been told I screw up every relationship I have. So maybe just do the opposite of what I'd do?

Well what would you do?

If I knew what I did wrong I'd stop! Zachary wrote. Then, after a minute, Probably. Another minute. I mean I'd try.

Wes snorted.

Kay going over there now. Later.

During the day?! It must be true love! Zachary wrote, then flooded Wes' screen with pink hearts.

Wes had hiked out to this spot once a week for the last six months, but he'd always gone at night. After all, you could only tell if lights were bright enough in the dark. And it had the added bonus of never bringing him in contact with people.

But seeing it in the daylight was a treat. They'd hung the fairy lights on Adam and Gus' house, and all agreed that it was almost to the point where they looked like they had the most lights in the whole world.

(Wes was glad he'd decided not to tell Gus about the Gay family of Lagrangeville, New York.)

In fact, Mr. Martinelli from next door commented on how glaringly bright the lights were as he stepped out to get his mail.

"Thank you!" Gus had called back.

Adam and Wes had snickered behind her back. Mr. Martinelli had narrowed his eyes at Wes and a flicker of unease had licked at Wes' stomach. It felt the same now as it had then, being observed. Anxious, vulnerable, squirmy.

"So, where's this clearing, then?" Adam asked after they'd walked for twenty minutes.

Gus had turned out to be an enthusiastic hiker after Wes' own heart, delighted by the footprints of animals and the bits of nature she kicked up as she walked, and prone to touching and smelling everything.

"About five more minutes," Wes told him.

"And how do you know this place?"

"I found it last year. I was looking for a spot where I could test out various bioluminescent apparatuses. But I needed somewhere far enough off the path that things wouldn't get disturbed, and someplace dark enough that there would be no light pollution. I checked out a lot of spots and this one was the best."

"What's light pollution?" Gus asked.

"It's when ambient light—light from the environment—reaches a spot. Like, light from people's houses or streetlights or buildings."

"You're trying to see if your bioluminescence will work to light this clearing?" Adam asked.

"Yes, basically. I'm trying to see how far each different illumination casts to understand how much of the biome would be required per square foot to light it."

They reached the clearing and Adam stopped short. Gus ran to examine things.

"What *is* this!?" she asked.

With a gentle finger, she traced the needles of the largest of the saplings Wes had planted.

"That's a Sunburst pine. That one is a Douglas fir. Those are blue spruce." He pointed to the ground in front of them. "These are Spartan junipers."

"They look weird," Gus said, screwing up her face and peering at them.

"Well, it's hard to see in the daylight. But they glow. If you cup your hand around a part of the plant, you can see it."

Wes used his larger hands to create enough darkness around Gus' eyes so she could see.

"Whoa! Did you do that?"

Wes nodded and Adam put a hand on his back.

"Can I see?"

Wes shaded Adam's eyes, too, and used the excuse to brush back his soft hair.

"Oh my god," Adam breathed. "You *made* trees glow? How?"

Satisfaction coursed through Wes. This was a project he'd begun at home, but he could quickly see that the laboratory setting, though generally useful for iterative experiments, wouldn't tell him if the glowing plants could survive in nature as well as in a hothouse. So he'd moved them out here in the spring, hoping the summer months would let them establish themselves sturdily enough in the environment that they'd survive the winter. He'd mulched them aggressively against the cold and so far they were doing well.

"In lay terms, if you can," Adam said.

Wes nodded. He was beginning to enjoy this new challenge of taking the complex processes he knew backward and forward and reimagining them in the simplest terms possible.

"You know how fireflies and algae glow?" Adam and Gus nodded. "I took the chemical that makes them glow and injected it into plants to see if they could make it part of themselves."

It had been eighteen months of painstaking experimentation, but that truly was the crux of it.

Adam was looking at him with a strange expression and Wes wondered if he hadn't simplified things enough.

"You're amazing." Adam shook his head. "That's amazing."

Wes ducked his head, self-conscious. "Thanks."

"Can I have a glowing tree?" Gus asked, eyes wide.

"Sweetie, this is Wes' research."

"I know," she said. "But maybe just a little one?"

Wes smiled. He'd thought she would be intrigued by his strange glowing trees.

"Maybe you can come over sometime and we can make you a glowing indoor plant, since it's winter."

"Really?!"

"Sure."

"I'm gonna have a glowing plant!" Gus sang to the trees around them. Then she plopped down beneath a nonglowing tree and began picking apart a pine cone.

"That's very sweet of you," Adam said, sliding his arm through Wes'. "You don't have to."

Wes knew he didn't have to. In fact, he'd spent the

last fifteen years of his life proving to himself over and over again that he didn't have to do a single god-damned thing he didn't want to do. Not anymore.

But he wanted to. Since he'd met Adam and Gus, he wanted to do something for someone else—reach outside the world of his home and connect with people for the first time in a long time.

"I want to," Wes said. "Maybe she'll get into plants because of it and give you a break with the spiders."

"Oh, bless you," Adam said, looking up at him with those mesmerizing blue eyes. "That would be a true Christmas miracle."

Chapter Seventeen

Adam

Adam had been forced to order several industrial power strips to accommodate all the lights they'd been sent for the house. Their electrical bill would be astronomical this month, but it didn't matter, because Gus' eyes lit up as bright as the house whenever she saw it.

Several people on Instagram had reposted his pictures and they'd gotten even more lights in the mail. Last night, when he put Gus to bed, instead of one of the stories he usually told her, she'd asked for the story of the magic lights.

"What do you mean, sweetie? Why don't you tell me the story?"

Gus snuggled into bed and told him the story.

"I wanted the most lights in the world, so you got tons of people to send us lights. We needed help with hanging them, and Wes helped us, and now you and Wes are gonna fall in love and he's gonna be with us all the time. So the lights have to be magic."

She'd been half asleep by the time she got to the end of the story, but that had heightened its impact rather than lessened it. Gus had never attributed anything to magic before. She'd always been exceedingly scientific—weirdly scientific for a child, truth be told. To hear her attribute Wes' presence in their life to magic showed Adam how very much she wanted a family Christmas.

And yes, Adam knew the two of them *were* a family, but clearly Gus wanted more.

It was a week until Gus' winter break started, ten days until Christmas, and Adam still had no present for her, and no idea if Mason would deign to even wish her a merry Christmas. He had considered texting Mason to ask, but couldn't even draft a message that wasn't razor-sharp.

Adam closed Gus' door and settled in front of *Meet Me in St. Louis* to brainstorm gift ideas for Gus.

"A video game console?" Charlie suggested at work the next day. "Kids like video games, right?"

"A bike?" Rye suggested. "I always wanted one when I was Gus' age."

"What presents would you have liked when you were eight, Marie?" Adam asked his mysterious coworker.

Marie's expression turned instantly mischievous and fond, but she just said mildly, "Does she like to read?"

"Could I put together a little laboratory for her or something?" Adam asked Wes that night after Gus was asleep.

Wes had come over for dinner and made lasagna about which Gus proclaimed, "Oh, weird, it's really good."

Adam gave her a look and she revised her sentiment.

"Sorry, I just meant, I didn't think you'd be able to cook but this is really good."

"Sweetie, it's not very nice to say that you assumed someone couldn't cook."

Gus cocked her head.

"Why?"

"Because making assumptions about people means that you are judging them based on what you believe, not what's true."

"Oh." She thought about that for a minute. "It's not bad to not be able to cook. You can't cook and you're awesome."

Adam smiled.

"Assumptions aren't necessarily bad. But what would you think if someone said they assumed you weren't good at science?"

"Why would someone think that? I'm great at science!" Gus said angrily.

"I know. It doesn't feel very good, huh?"

"Sorry, Wes," Gus said. "I didn't mean to make you feel bad."

"Thanks," Wes said. "Why *did* you assume I couldn't cook?"

Gus ate a huge bite of lasagna and chewed thoughtfully. Adam had worked very hard to teach her to be open to questions and not get defensive. He watched proudly as she really considered the question.

"I guess cuz your house is full of weird stuff and cooking's such a normal thing. I thought you maybe wouldn't care about it."

Wes nodded. "That makes a lot of sense. Good lesson that a real scientist can't extrapolate too much."

"What's that?"

"It means a scientist can't take one piece of data they know and make the mistake of thinking it also means another piece of data they don't know."

"I want to be a real scientist," Gus said softly.

"Well, now you know one way to be an even better one," Wes said, and held up his hand.

Gus high-fived it.

"Thanks," she told him, like he'd given her a gift. Then she shoved more lasagna in her mouth.

Adam looked at Wes, his heart so full he could hardly stand it. Wes winked at him and pressed his knee to Adam's under the table.

Now, after cleaning up the kitchen, they were in the living room, fire once again crackling merrily on the television screen.

"A laboratory…" Wes mused. "Maybe. Depends what you mean. My eight-year-old self would kill me for saying so, but I think she's probably too young for an actual chemistry set with, you know, chemicals."

Adam's heart lurched, imagining his baby getting burned with acid or spattered in…something else corrosive.

"Yeah, no chemicals, definitely not. Um. What else is in a laboratory?"

"Fire."

Adam blanched.

"Just kidding," Wes said. "I mean, there *is* fire, but—"

"Yeah, yeah, yeah, I get it, a laboratory is basically a death trap. Never mind."

Adam deflated.

"I just. I know it's silly. I know the perfect holiday gift won't really…make Gus forget stuff with Mason or leaving Boulder. I just want this Christmas to be great. I want Gus to be happy and see that this is a good move for us and that we're gonna be okay and, and, and…"

He gestured broadly, like he could pluck the words out of the air.

Wes caught his hands and brought them to his lips, kissing the knuckles of each. His eyes were warm and intense and Adam wanted to let himself drown in them.

"You're already doing everything to help Gus feel that way," he said, soft and sure. "You're thinking about what is best for her. You've practically buried your house alive in lights because she asked for it. And most important, you're here. You're spending time with her. That's what makes it feel like a holiday. That's what makes it special."

Wes' eyes grew shadowed.

"At least, I assume so."

"Your family didn't spend time together at the holidays?"

Wes snorted.

"The holidays were just an excuse for my dad to throw huge, lavish cocktail parties for all the people he wanted to impress. He and my mom would spend months planning every detail of the food, the drinks, the music, their outfits, and then they'd spend the entire party pretending it was effortless. Lana and I had to be there, dressed to the nines, so they could show us off like ornaments on a tree. But when the guests were gone and the music was turned off, all we had for Christmas was a fridge full of leftover hors d'oeuvres and a pile of fancy, impersonal gifts from strangers."

Wes shrugged, his eyes flat.

"And now?" Adam asked.

"Now?"

"Yeah, now that you can do whatever you want, how do you celebrate?"

"Oh. I don't, really. At all. Anything."

"How come?"

Wes traced Adam's cheek absently, and when he spoke his voice was husky and low.

"I guess I never felt like I had much to celebrate."

Adam felt the words like they'd been thrown at him, and they hurt.

Wes—beautiful, brilliant, sweet, generous, weird-in-a-great-way Wes—didn't feel like he had anything to celebrate.

Adam's mission was clear: he had to celebrate the hell out of Westley Mobray.

"Well that's settled, then," Adam said, forgetting he hadn't said any of that out loud.

"What's settled?"

"You should have Christmas with us!"

For a moment, Adam thought Wes didn't like the idea. Maybe it was too soon? Mason had always told him he got too invested, too enthusiastic, jumped the gun. But it felt *right* to Adam—so right. And when things felt right, he wanted more of them.

Then Adam realized that Wes had turned away and was clenching his fists because he didn't want Adam to see the emotion in his face.

"Come here," Adam said. He tugged Wes back to him. "Look at me."

Wes raised his eyes to Adam's. His nostrils flared and he licked his lips, and Adam could see the years of solitude and isolation crumble like a cliff face into the sea.

"I— If you— Really?"

Adam's heart swelled with affection for Wes. He wanted to pull him so tight against his chest that he could feel Wes' heartbeat and the movement of each breath. He wanted to kiss him and kiss him until all they could taste was each other. He wanted to sleep and wake and sleep and wake with Wes' arms around him and his arms around Wes, and *shit*, Adam knew what that meant.

He knew what it meant and he knew it was too soon and *Adam, gah, don't say it out loud!* he screamed at himself. But even if he didn't say it, he knew: he was falling for Wes Mobray. Seriously, deeply, no joke falling in love with him.

Love. *Shit*.

Chapter Eighteen

Wes

Adam Mills had invited him for Christmas.

It was such an ordinary sentence, but it set Wes' blood on fire with joy and possibility.

His senior year of high school had been the last time he'd attended his parents' annual holiday cocktail party. He'd made the obligatory appearance, endured the endless comments about his stint on *The Edge of Day*, and ducked every offer from an agent or casting director to get him back in the spotlight. The spotlight was, he explained, exactly what he wanted to escape.

The next year, he'd stayed at Caltech through winter break, making excuses about needing to monitor his experiments in the lab, and he did so for the next three years too, until he graduated. When he started back at Caltech as a grad student, he stopped going home to visit altogether. The invitations became perfunctory, then. More an excuse for his parents and Lana to express their disappointment and hurt than any genuine desire to see him (or so Wes believed).

Every now and then over the years someone in his

cohort would drag him to a holiday party. They were a relief of cheap drinks and frozen hors d'oeuvres and white elephant gifts with budgets of ten dollars or less. But although they were less stressful, he didn't enjoy them. Just like his parents' parties, they reminded him that he didn't belong; just in a different way.

One year, he was dating Lyle seriously enough that he agreed to accompany him home for the holidays. It had been an exercise in torment because Lyle had told his parents about Wes' family and they took advantage of any downtime by asking him to tell them stories of Hollywood and what it was like to be on a film set. He looked at Lyle differently after that. He'd been the first person in grad school that Wes had confided in about his family and he'd thought Lyle understood how reticent he was to be connected with them. After all, he'd enrolled in grad school under his mother's last name precisely to distance himself from his past, his father, and now his sister, because Lana's star was also on the rise.

Lyle had blinked wide eyes and apologized, but said he thought his family would be so interested that he'd been sure Wes wouldn't mind slaking their curiosity.

Wes hadn't left in the middle of the trip because he abhorred drama of all kinds. But he'd quietly ended the relationship in his mind right then and there, and ended it out loud a week later when they returned to Pasadena.

He hadn't celebrated a holiday since.

Occasionally on his birthday, he'd buy himself some piece of gear he'd wanted for his work, but he did that not on his birthday as well. And he never, ever, ever acknowledged Christmas (although he enjoyed Zachary's seasonal texts repurposing cheesy Christmas memes into Chanukah ones).

But this year...

This year, he wouldn't be alone.

This year, Christmas wouldn't pass unnoticed and unacknowledged.

This year, he had two people to share it with. Two people who gleamed like bright stars in the darkness.

Wes stroked Bettie's back as he began to dream up the gift he would give to Adam and Gus. It wasn't impossible, but it would be a time crunch. He decided to put on another pot of coffee and get down to business.

"Daddy says you're having Christmas with us—is it true!?"

Wes had opened the door at Gus' enthusiastic bell ringing, and found her cheeks flushed and Adam waving from across the street.

"Come on in," Wes said, saluting Adam and giving him a wink over Gus' head.

She was there, as agreed, to create her glowing plant.

"But is it true, Wes?!"

She bounced inside and shoved her hands in her pockets, something Adam had taught her to do when she got so excited she wanted to tug on people to get their attention.

Wes grinned. She was so freaking cute.

"Yeah, it's true. That okay with you?"

"It's perfection!" Gus trilled, spinning around, and Wes couldn't help agreeing with her.

"Cool."

"Cool," she echoed. "Cool, cool, cool!"

She was practically vibrating with excitement as she skipped after him to the living room where he'd laid out everything they would need.

He was going to be showing Gus how to flood the plant with the luciferase enzyme instead of splicing it into the plant's DNA as Wes had done with the trees he planted in the clearing. He had a feeling Gus was far more interested in quick results than long-lasting ones.

He had packaged luciferase, luciferin, and coenzyme A in nanoparticles to help each one get to the right part of the plant, and suspended them in a solution.

"Okay, so we're going to take your plant and put it in this tube. The tube is full of a solution I made that is what will make the plant glow."

Gus nodded, eyes wide.

"Do you know what kind of plant this is?" Wes asked her.

She shook her head.

"It's kale."

She wrinkled her nose. "Do you eat that?"

"Yeah. It's a very hardy plant that can grow in lots of different environments. If you put it in your window, even in the winter, the cold won't bother it."

She nodded.

"This is an autoclave. It's gonna pressurize the solution, which will allow the particles that hold the glowing agent to enter tiny pores in the plants, called stomata."

He tapped his own face.

"Pores are like what we have in our skin. They let our skin breathe. It's the same with plants. Basically. Once the particles have entered the stomata, it will begin to glow."

Gus' eyes were huge.

He showed her how to put the kale plant into the solution, then turned on the autoclave, and they watched the plant slowly darken as the solution was pushed in through the stomata.

"Whoa," Gus breathed.

"It'll take a bit before it starts glowing," Wes said, not wanting her to be disappointed.

"Okay. Can we take it to my house so Daddy can see it too?"

"Sure."

She was so excited about the soon-to-be-glowing plant that she only called hello and goodbye to Bettie and the other animals, before grabbing Wes' hand and pulling him to the door.

"Just grab my coat," he said, managing to snag it with one hand before he was encouraged out the door.

"Sorry." Gus grimaced and waited impatiently as he pulled it on.

She shielded the kale plant inside her own jacket for the walk across the street, hugging it to her chest against the cold.

She reminded Wes so much of himself sometimes.

"Daddy!" she yelled as they got inside. "I made a plant glow!" She paused and looked back at Wes. "Wes helped," she added, and Wes smiled.

Adam came out of the kitchen with an adorable smear of flour on his cheek.

Wes' eyes got wide.

"Oh, no. Daddy. Are you baking?" She asked it with the horror usually reserved for questions like "Was it malignant?" or "Is it contagious?"

Adam laughed.

"Never fear. It's slice and bake cookies. I just used a little flour to roll out the dough. I got Christmas cookie cutters. Wanna help?"

Plant instantly abandoned in Wes' hands, Gus made a beeline for the kitchen.

"Hi," Adam said. "How'd it go?"

"Good. I'll just put this in her room, if that's okay?"

"Sure." Adam studied it. "Is it really going to glow?"

"It should."

Adam shook his head.

"Jesus. You're seriously unbelievable, do you know that?"

The word had been levied at Wes before, yes, but never in the extremely fond, slightly awed tone that infused Adam's voice.

Wes caught his elbow and drew him close. Adam smelled of sugar and Wes wanted to see if he tasted like it too. He leaned in and kissed Adam's soft lips. They tasted as sweet as he smelled and Wes sank into Adam's warmth.

Kissing Adam felt like home.

"Daddy, can I make a Christmas monster!?" Gus called from the kitchen.

"Sure, sweetie."

Adam kissed Wes one more time.

"I'll meet you in the kitchen," Wes said, running his fingers through the hair at Adam's nape.

Wes settled the kale on Gus' windowsill, adjusting the blinds to make sure it would get enough sun. It was a western-facing window, but maybe he'd bring a clip-on plant light over tomorrow if it didn't seem like the winter sun was enough.

Gus' room was a tornado of bits and pieces of things she'd clearly taken apart, or found, or taken off of other appliances. She had a screwdriver, a pair of needle-nose pliers, and a spool of floral wire next to a pile of rivets in a drawer, and everywhere were books, flopped open on their spines and flagged with bits of torn paper as bookmarks. Wes felt like he'd wandered back in time to his own childhood bedroom—although that had been ruthlessly ordered once a week by the cleaning lady his parents employed. In between, though, Wes collected piles of this and that to experiment with, and consulted books for guidance.

He truly didn't mean to snoop. He was just curious if he could get a sense of what she might be making.

On her desk lay an unfinished letter, written in Gus' chaotic scrawl.

I know you don't exist, it said, *but just in case you do, will you make Wes stay? Daddy and me are so happy now and I want us to be a family.*

The letter was addressed to *Nicholas Santa Claus*.

Wes froze, awash in conflicting emotions. First and most superficial: fear. The fear that someone needing him would end up the way it had the last time, when his father had needed him. With their relationship in tatters and Wes guilty and miserable.

But when he dug a little deeper there was also hope. That maybe this time, being needed didn't mean doing something he didn't want, but participating in something he did. He adored Gus. And his feelings for Adam grew stronger every hour they spent together.

He took deep breaths through his nose and blew them out his mouth, and slowly, the fear dissipated. He reread the letter and focused on the hope.

Daddy and me are so happy now. So happy.

So was Wes. And if Gus and Adam were happy and so was he…then…

Wes walked into the kitchen where Gus and Adam stood at the kitchen table. Backs to Wes, their blond hair similarly messy, they had their arms around each other and were concentrating on something on the table.

Wes was filled with such overwhelming affection that he felt his nose tickle and his eyes prick with tears. He put a hand on each of their shoulders and peered over their heads. On the table was…something made out of dough.

"Is that, um…what is that?"

"It's a Christmas monster!" Gus said gleefully.

Adam smiled up at him.

"It eats Christmas lights and then it glows, just like my plant. See?"

She pointed and Wes could vaguely make out a blob that might've been fairy lights around what might've been the midsection of the creature.

"Got it," Wes said.

"It'll be better when I frost it," Gus assured him.

Over the next two hours they cut out dozens of shapes—Gus had eschewed the cookie cutters immediately, claiming that snowflakes and reindeer were boring, and Wes was inclined to agree with her. They made monsters that ate Christmas trees and Christmas trees that ate monsters. Santa Clauses that were half lizard and half human and tarantula elves. (Adam shuddered at them even in dough form.)

As the cookies baked, they tinted frosting with food coloring and Adam spooned it into plastic bags he cut the tips off of to make piping bags. "I saw it on Pinterest," he explained, and Gus started chatting before Wes could ask what Pinterest was.

To get them the colors they wanted, the frosting ended up a bit runny, so when Wes tried to use green frosting to outline the tree his monster was eating, it mixed with the red frosting he'd used to frost the monster, resulting in a gloppy brown mess that looked less like a monster and more like what you might do if you saw one.

Adam's and Gus' didn't look much better—in fact, truth be told, Adam's looked much worse—but no one cared. Adam had put on Christmas music and while outside the snow was coming down in freezing gusts, the kitchen was oven warm and cheery, all of them laughing as Gus launched a monster attack where one of her tree-eating monsters became a tree-eating-monster eater and demolished Wes' tree-eating monster, smashing both to a sugary paste that she scooped up and ate with her fingers.

"Monsters are so yummy," she said an hour later, tongue, teeth, and lips an unearthly blue-green color from the dye in the frosting. She was tired and crashing from the sugar, so Adam got a peanut butter sandwich in her and then put her to bed, claiming that the food coloring would come off on its own eventually.

Wes cleaned up the kitchen while Adam settled Gus in, getting blue-and-red fingertips for his trouble, and made some mint tea.

When Adam came back in the kitchen he draped himself over Wes' shoulders and squeezed him.

"You angel," he murmured, and kissed his neck. "Thank you for cleaning up. You really didn't have to."

"'S okay," Wes murmured.

Christmas music still issued faintly from Adam's phone, a tinkly song Wes recognized but couldn't name. He stood and pulled Adam against him, rocking to the rhythm of the song. With Adam's cheek on his chest and his arms around him, Wes felt perfectly at peace.

The wind whistled outside, but Adam was warm and smelled so good. They were half dancing, half swaying, and went on that way for a song and a half, until the music cut out and Adam swore.

"Phone died," he muttered.

"Doesn't matter," Wes said.

They settled in the living room with their tea.

"Guess what," Adam said.

"Hmm?"

"The plant was glowing just a bit when I turned the light off."

"Oh, good. I was worried it might not work and she'd be disappointed."

"She was really excited. She wanted to come back out and show you but I made her go to bed."

Wes hummed with quiet satisfaction.

"Can I ask you something?"

"Mmm-hmm, anything."

"I don't know how to say it exactly, so forgive me, but, do you do things with what you create? Like, do you sell them to someone? Are you employed by someone?"

"I'm still in the experimentation phase, mainly," Wes said carefully.

Adam's question had been gentle, if clumsy, but Adam was not the first one to point out that Wes hadn't actually *done* anything yet.

"I didn't mean to be mean about it," Adam said, putting a hand on his arm and sounding so much like Gus that Wes smiled.

He shook his head.

"Not mean. I...I know it's weird that I just work out of my house. I, um. I had a job offer a few years ago, but it wasn't a good fit."

He'd had many over the years, in fact, all contingent on compromising his research in order to rush to sale.

"I got a big grant in my last year of grad school and that's what I used to initially fund most of my research. But since then, I've used the money I had in the bank from *Edge of Day*. I didn't like to use it, but all the companies that are interested in biolumi-nescence want me to design a product for them to sell rather than just funding research. There's a lot of money in green marketing. A lot of people who will pay handsomely for alternative energy and feel like they're offsetting their carbon footprint or whatever."

Wes rolled his eyes.

"But I'm not interested in selling it. Not like that, anyway. My goal isn't to make glow-in-the-dark nightlight plants for Pasadena kindergarteners. This science could rewrite the way we use energy, period. Did you know lighting accounts for twenty percent of worldwide energy consumption? Sorry, did I already tell you that? Anyway, it's huge."

Adam nodded.

"And that usage is public as well as private. And on the public side of things, there are huge discrepancies in where lighting is used. There are neighborhoods in LA where you could read a book in the middle of the night—rich, heavily surveilled neighborhoods. Then there are ones where the streetlights got smashed or burned out years ago and were never replaced. Or where the city just stopped routing electricity to lights altogether. It's the same in every city in the country. Poor neighborhoods, neighborhoods the city government considers dangerous or unimportant, they don't get the same budget for lighting, which makes them *more* dangerous, less desirable. And on and on."

"I saw it in Boulder too," Adam agreed.

"Or rural areas where houses are too far apart for the county to want to light the road—they have so many collisions with animals or other cars. But imagine if we could light those neighborhoods the cities underserve, or those rural roads the county has dismissed, with something that is self-sustaining and doesn't require any fabricated energy source, like trees. It could revolutionize the way people experience their environments."

Adam threw himself into Wes' lap and kissed him.

"You're so damn hot," Adam said. "Seriously, you're just amazing."

"I…thank you," Wes stammered, not knowing what to say to that.

"Would you ever want to— Never mind."

"What?"

Wes cupped Adam's face.

"Nah, you just said you wanted to revolutionize the world. This isn't that."

"Tell me."

"Well, it's really small, but… I was talking with one of the other parents at Gus' school the other day when I dropped her off, and in the winter, the bus stop for her daughter is dark because the sun rises so late. So she waits with her because it's kind of scary in the dark. I guess I was thinking maybe there was a way to light them. Never mind," he said again.

"Hmm."

Wes immediately began parsing what would and would not work, filing away the former and rejecting the latter, narrowing to a plan.

Adam said, "Wes? Are you mad?"

"Huh? No, course not."

"Oh. You're frowning."

"Sorry, just thinking," Wes said. "Where is the bus stop?"

"I'm not sure what road, exactly, but I can ask Caroline next time I see her."

Wes nodded, already miles ahead.

"Maybe I can get a map of the bus stops from the school district. If I overlay a map of the lighting grid from the Department of Energy, I can see which stops would be in darkness starting on which day of the year, given sunrise times, then I could—"

Adam cut him off with his mouth, kissing him passionately.

Wes laughed and kissed him back.

"Too much detail?" he asked.

Adam nodded. "You're amazing. Now shut up and kiss me."

Wes was happy to oblige.

Chapter Nineteen

Adam

The day had started out perfectly. Adam had woken in Wes' arms with Wes nuzzling his neck, then Wes had slid beneath the covers, pressed kisses to the sensitive skin of his inner thighs, and then brought Adam to transcendent orgasm, light bursting behind his eyes and shock waves of pleasure rolling over his whole body.

Matheson's Hardware was cheerily busy all day, customers buying tools and fixings to hang decorations and searching for the perfect aid for their last-minute holiday projects.

Rye had even come in to help out for the day, though he mostly seemed to swear at the cash register as it jammed or spat out long scrolls of tape. During one lunchtime lull, he regaled Adam and a customer with the tale of his own failed DIY, which he'd meant to be a laptop desk for Charlie, but which had turned out a hunched and mangled hunk of wood so covered in glue that Charlie deemed it unsafe even to burn in effigy.

Adam was laughing at this when Charlie came

out of the office and gave him a questioning look. Rye simply said mournfully, "Laptop desk. RIP," and Charlie snorted and pulled Rye against his side in a tight hug.

As he drove home, Adam got a text from Wes that said, You're so lovely. Thanks for liking me, and was moved to tears. How very like Wes to thank him for that.

At a stoplight he texted back a string of heart emojis, and sighed happily, turning the radio to a station playing Christmas music. He'd even had an idea for Gus' Christmas gift. His heart was very, very full.

He was trying (and failing for the thousandth time) to whistle a Christmas carol as he walked in the front door, planning what to make for dinner and wondering if Wes would want to come over again tonight.

Shoes off, Adam paused. The house was oddly silent. Usually when he got home from work, the television was on or Gus was laughing or River was talking. But now, nothing.

"Hello?"

River came into the living room, looking drawn, and Adam's heart felt like it leapt to his throat.

"What is it, what's wrong, what happened?"

River squeezed his arm.

"She's fine," they said immediately. "She's just… uhh."

Adam pulled River down on the couch, his entire being desperate to hear what had happened.

If one of those little shits hurt my baby I will rend them limb from limb!

But before River could explain, Adam's phone rang. It was Gus' school. He showed the screen to River, whose eyes went wide.

"Yeah, yeah, get it. I'll see you later."

They waved and were out the door.

Adam answered the phone, a pit forming in his stomach as he listened to the principal.

"Mr. Mills, August is a delightful child. She's engaged and curious, and quite an, er, critical thinker. It's the last of these that I need to talk with you about. I've had multiple calls from parents about an incident that transpired today with August. It would seem she made an announcement on the playground during recess that Santa Claus does not exist."

Oh, Gus.

"She was *quite* insistent about it, even after it clearly upset several of the other children. Now," Mrs. Gordon said gently, "Of course it is up to each family what they teach their children, but as I'm sure you're aware, the timing of the Santa-isn't-real discussion is something that most parents want to choose for themselves."

Adam pinched the bridge of his nose, feeling a headache threatening.

"Gosh, I'm really sorry. I get that, of course. I'm not sure what I can do, though," he said honestly.

The loud sigh on the other end of the call rather suggested that Mrs. Gordon also didn't know what there was to be done.

"Perhaps a conversation with August about which are at-home conversations and which are at-school conversations."

Adam rubbed deeply into the spot between his eyebrows.

"Yeah, I can do that," he said. "But Gus is eight. Eight-year-olds are gonna say what they're gonna say, and there really doesn't seem to be a power on earth that can stop them. I've tried. I'm sure there were plenty of kids saying that Santa *does* exist. So…"

He shrugged even though she couldn't see him.

"There were *tears*, Mr. Mills. *Phone calls*."

Adam sighed.

"Yeah, I get it. My kid made your life harder by being a kid. But Gus isn't who your problem is with. It's with the parents who are bothering you. It is up to all of them what they tell their kids and when. But it's not up to Gus—an *eight-year-old*—to manage that for them. Part of living in the world is that people are different and believe different things. It's not bad for those kids to learn that lesson, even if their parents apparently haven't."

"Mr. Mills," she began, placatingly. "If August could just tell the other children that she was joking—"

Sometimes Adam forgot, because he was an adult now, and in charge of his life, but he was back in Garnet Run. Back in the town that he'd spent eighteen years of his life in. Back in the town where his classmates had tormented him for being different, for being sensitive, for having the gall to want a life beyond its borders. He knew this place, even if it had been over a decade since he'd left. And there was no way he was having his child go through what he had.

"I'm sorry, but no. I grew up in Garnet Run. I know

what it's like. But you are a *public* school. Those kids' parents can teach them whatever they want at home, but so can I. I'm sorry that you're having to deal with these parents, but I imagine if it wasn't about Gus, they'd be calling you about something else. I am absolutely not going to ask my daughter to lie. Period. I don't see this conversation bringing about any more useful solutions, so I'm going to end it."

Adam hung up the phone, wishing his cell phone was a landline so he could've slammed it for emphasis.

"Small-minded piece of shit conservative fu—"

Adam cut himself off when he saw Gus standing wide-eyed in the doorway. Her face was blotchy and tear streaked.

"Am I in trouble?" she asked timidly, and crept into the living room.

"No way," Adam said fiercely. "But we did talk about how it's unkind to tell other kids that Santa isn't real if they're still enjoying the magic of him. I know we say no lying. But make believe isn't the same as lying. And sometimes we choose to believe things because they bring us joy or comfort."

Gus hung her head.

"The truth is important. But kindness is important too. And taking away someone's joy or comfort isn't kind."

"I know."

"Why'd you do it, then?"

Gus sulked her way to the couch.

"Tommy VanderHaag said Santa was bringing him a new mom for Christmas cuz his dad's getting married. I told him that wasn't Santa, that was a wedding. And he said…" She scowled. "He said, what did I know cuz I didn't even have a mom."

Adam's heart broke for her, but Gus went on.

"So I said, of *course* I have a mom, I just live with my dad and what did *he* know because Santa didn't even exist. It just slipped out! And then a lot of other kids came over and they started saying Santa *was* real and I got mad, so I told them the evidence."

Adam surreptitiously rubbed at his temples where the headache had spread.

Just then, a text came from Wes: You guys okay over there?

Adam's eyes went wide.

How'd you know something was up?

What's wrong?! Do you need help??

Then Wes added, It's the first day Gus hasn't turned the lights on the second she got home from school.

Tears stung Adam's eyes. Wes paid attention. Wes cared.

It's okay. Gus just had a hard day, Adam wrote. She got in trouble at school and it's UNJUST.

Wes sent a quizzical face emoji. I'm here if you need me.

Adam sent a heart and wrote, I'll tell you everything in a bit.

"Is that Wes?"

"Yeah."

"Wes would agree with me."

"That Santa isn't real? I'm sure he would." Gus looked triumphant. "The thing is, sweetie… Here, come in the kitchen while I make dinner."

Adam rubbed his head harder, trying to think of how to say this.

"There's science-y real and then there's the other kind of real. A story can be real, even a fantasy story, because it lets you understand things that strictly real reality doesn't."

"Like what?" Gus asked, of course, because Adam didn't have an answer.

"Um, like…like what happens after we die. No one really knows. But stories that explore different possibilities can be useful and comforting, even if they're just things to think about."

Adam rummaged through the cabinets trying to find where Wes had filed the rice, because it wasn't under *R*. He found it under *B*, for basmati.

"The point is that sometimes there are things that aren't true, but truth isn't the point of them. And Santa Claus is one of those things. It's like a…a collective story that we participate in because it can be fun and magical. Like, what makes Christmas so great? The feeling, right? It feels cozy and exciting and special because it's about family and love. When we give someone a gift, it shows we're thinking about them and what they would like. When we share a special meal or a ritual, it's creating something that's just for our family or friends. Something that brings us closer together. That feels good." Gus nodded reluctantly. "Sometimes," Adam said, tipping her chin up and kissing her forehead, "feeling cozy and loved and together is more important than scientific truth."

The doorbell rang after dinner and Wes ducked inside, shaking snow off his hat.

"Wes!" Gus cried, spirit undampened.

"Hey, Gus. I heard you had a rough day so I brought someone to spend the night with you. She's, uh, in the entryway."

Wes winked at Gus and her eyes got wide.

"I'll keep her in the box this time," she whispered completely audibly.

Wes had texted Adam earlier to see if he could stand having Bettie in the house and Adam had told him he'd feel a lot better if he had Bettie *and* Wes. Wes had replied with a heart emoji.

As Gus ran for the entryway, Wes held up a bag to Adam.

"I also brought ice cream, for those less excited about Bettie."

Adam smiled and Wes crossed to him and pulled him into his arms.

"You okay?" Wes asked. He stroked Adam's hair.

"Yeah. Thanks."

"What kind did you bring?" Gus asked, face bright. Bettie seemed to have revived her completely.

Wes put the bag on the table. "Check it out."

Gus' eyes got wider and wider as she pulled six different kinds of ice cream out of the bag.

"Wow," she breathed worshipfully.

Adam shook his head but squeezed Wes' hand.

"I wasn't sure what you liked," Wes said.

Gus seemed to be trying to hold all the containers at once.

"One bowl," Adam said, perusing the selection himself.

Gus considered each flavor seriously and then said, "One bowl or one flavor?"

"Go to town, kid," Adam said, and Gus did a little dance of excitement. She then proceeded to put some of every flavor in the bowl.

Adam helped himself to some mint chocolate chip. Wes took the salted caramel. They settled in the living room and Adam put the fire on.

"Oh, Dad," Gus said, like this amused her.

"Oh, Gus," Adam replied. "How's that combination of lemon sorbet and peanut butter cup treating you?"

Gus took a big bite and mushed it around in her mouth a little.

Adam cringed.

Gus swallowed and grinned.

"Pretty good," she declared.

Wes shuddered.

"Ah, to be young and unburdened by taste," Adam said.

Gus ate her Frankenstein ice cream happily for a while and then turned her attention to Wes.

"Why aren't you having Christmas with your family?" she asked.

Wes put his bowl down and addressed her seriously.

"Well, because I don't get along with my parents or my sister. I haven't seen them in years. You're supposed to spend time with people who make you happy. But my family makes me feel bad. So I don't spend time with them."

Gus wrinkled her brow.

"Did they leave?"

"No. I left. I choose not to spend time with them."

Gus' mouth formed an O, like she didn't know you could do that.

"Are you sad?" she asked.

"Nope. I'm happier not seeing them."

"Oh."

She thought about that for a while.

"I bet they're sad."

Wes' face did something complicated.

"Why do you say that?"

Gus shrugged like it was obvious.

"You're awesome. Too bad for them that they made you stay away."

Wes blinked and Gus dropped her spoon into her empty bowl with a sigh.

"Well, I'm tired," she announced, stretching dramatically. "Guess I'll go to bed early."

It was one minute before her bedtime so the pronouncement had less impact than she might have intended.

"Hey, thanks, Gus," Wes said. He looked a little dazed.

She smiled.

"Night."

* * *

Adam woke to eighty-three mentions on Instagram. Even when he'd used Instagram to try and drum up attention for his work he'd never woken to eighty-three mentions.

Wes had kissed him goodbye and gone home a few minutes earlier because Adam thought it would be good for Gus to have a low-key morning, given the events of the day before.

Blearily, Adam tapped the screen.

His most recent shot of himself and Gus in front of their lit-up house had apparently been shared under the hashtag WinterInWyoming and then landed in several people's stories. One of them, an account with a million followers that comprised images of cozy cabins with roaring fires, mugs of cocoa cupped by mittened hands, and winter trees glazed with icicle lights, had shared the picture along with hands making a heart and a string of lights gif, commenting, "Dad and daughter Xmas goals. Adorable!!"

That account seemed to be the source of most of the shares. He liked the posts and reposted the stories, thrilled to show Gus.

He took his phone into her room and gently stroked her hair to wake her up.

"Morning, baby. Wanna see something cool?"

Gus nodded, instantly awake. She could never resist a line like that.

Adam showed her the reposted photograph and she flipped through the mentions expertly.

"Oh my god," she breathed. "Are we famous?"

Adam laughed.

"Nah, but people seem to think we're kinda cool."

He winked at her in an aggressively uncool way and she laughed.

"Wish I had a phone so I could show people at school," she said innocently.

Adam took a moment to bask in his utter relief that Gus did not have a phone, because he could only imagine the things she would show her classmates in the interest of scientific rigor.

"Listen, about the kids at school."

Adam had spent a long time thinking about the situation the night before and had come to a conclusion that satisfied him. Somehow, snugged tight in Wes' arms, everything had seemed less galling. In fact, when Adam told Wes the whole story, complete with Gus' Martin Luther nailing the ninety-five theses of Why Santa Obviously Doesn't Exist to the door, Wes cracked up.

"I want you to let them believe whatever they believe about Santa. No, wait. Listen," he said as she started to open her mouth. "You don't know what everyone's situation is, or what they do at home. Some kids like to believe in magic and Santa Claus and the Tooth Fairy because it makes them happy, just like science and truth make you happy. It's not okay for you to force your beliefs on anyone—period."

Gus wrinkled her brows.

"Yes, baby, some people think science is a belief.

So if there are kids who want to talk about it with you and they're okay with Santa not existing, then fine. But it's not your place to try and convince anyone if they want to believe. This is really important. I need you to promise me. You won't try and force your beliefs on anyone."

"Okay," Gus sighed. "I won't."

Adam had extracted one more promise from Gus when he dropped her off at school—this one a pinkie promise, that most sacred of vows—not to argue about Santa. And he considered it a good sign that he didn't get any phone calls during the day, either from irate parents or from Gus' principal.

Just before he finished work, though, River texted, NBD but text me when you can.

At Adam's expression, Marie waved for him to go, so Adam called them back as he tidied up the shelves in aisle two.

"Is something wrong? Is Gus okay?"

"Dude, we need a code word that I'll use if something is actually wrong. You raise my blood pressure every time you do this."

"Sorry, sorry," Adam said. "What's up?"

"Just, there are a *lot* of packages on your driveway. Gus wanted to open them when we got home. She said you guys are famous now? I didn't want her to, in case… I dunno. In case there was something weird in any of them. I just wanted to let you know."

"Have I told you lately that you're the best sibling in the whole world and that I appreciate you so much?" Adam said.

River made a predictably dismissive sound.

"Seriously, River. I could not be here without you."

"Aw," River said. They sounded pleased.

Suddenly Adam realized how close it was to Christmas and that he hadn't discussed it with River yet.

"Do you need to be with the cats on Christmas, or can you come over?" Adam asked.

There was a pause, then River said, "Yeah? Really?"

Crushing guilt lodged in Adam's stomach. He'd been so concerned about Gus and himself that he'd forgotten to invite River until now.

"Of course! I'm so sorry I didn't ask you before now. I've been a little…"

He made a scattered gesture that River couldn't see.

"No worries."

"No, seriously. You've been here for me and I've been really self-involved. I'm sorry. I'm gonna do better. But of course I want you to come. And Gus would love it. Also, um, you know Wes…from across the street? He might come too."

"For real?" They dropped their voice. "So it's going well?"

Adam grinned into a tub of hex bolts. "So damn well."

River's voice was tender.

"I'm really happy for you."

"Thanks. So you'll come, then?"

"Yeah, okay."

Adam hung up the phone with a solemn vow that he would be better about making sure he was there for River just as they'd been there for him.

Chapter Twenty

Adam

It had taken Adam and Wes hours yesterday, under Gus' watchful directorship, but they had finally hung all the lights that had been dropped off.

"Can't believe you put your home address on Instagram," Wes had muttered halfway through.

Adam had agreed. Originally he'd thought maybe two or three people might drop off lights. He hadn't been worried about his privacy—this was Garnet Run, Wyoming, population five thousand on a populous day, where people left each other alone.

With people sharing the post, though... He'd opened his original post and edited it to remove his address.

It was five days until Christmas. Adam figured people had better things to do than concern themselves with his lights.

"Daddy!"

"In the kitchen! Do you want oatmeal or waffles?"

"Daddy, look!"

Adam took a slug of his coffee and wiped eyes bleary from another late night with Wes. *Totally worth it.*

Adam followed Gus' voice to the front door and found her face pressed to the window.

Outside, their neighbor Mr. Montgomery was pointing at their house and talking to two strangers, bundled up against the cold. One of them raised her phone and snapped a picture of the house.

"Stay here," Adam instructed.

He pulled on a coat and stepped into his boots.

"Can I help you?" he asked.

"Hi! I'm sorry," the woman who'd taken the picture said, smiling. "I saw your picture on Instagram and I wanted to see the lights you and your little girl hung. It's such a sweet story. Guess it was silly to come during the day."

She looked sheepish.

Adam could imagine what Wes would say if he were here. He'd mutter, "Well, certainly don't come prowling around my house at *night*."

But Adam wasn't Wes, and the idea that a real-life person had been moved by Gus' wish for the most lights in the world filled him with warmth.

"That's okay. Hi, I'm Adam."

"I'm Naomi," the woman said. "That's my brother, Jordan." She pointed to the guy getting something out of their car. "We brought you these."

Jordan gave a self-conscious wave as he turned around. He was holding two coils of lights.

"Hey," he said. "Thought maybe you all could use some more."

He held out the lights and Adam swallowed a lump in his throat.

"Wow," he breathed.

"We know it's a little weird that we came here," Naomi said. "It's just, um. Our parents used to get really into Christmas. Tons of lights and decorations and all. Our mom died a few years ago and last year our dad had a heart attack. He can't really be climbing on ladders to hang lights anymore. When I saw your post it just reminded me so much of when we were kids."

Naomi gave a sad smile and Jordan squeezed her hand.

"It's really cool, you doing this for your daughter," he said.

Adam was desperately holding back tears, not wanting to make these kind strangers uncomfortable.

"Thank you," he choked out. "That's really so kind of you. And I'm sorry about your parents. I wish—"

He broke off, tears too close to the surface.

"Ignore me," he said, waving a hand in front of his face as if that might disappear the tears.

"Daddy!" Gus came running up behind him and wrapped her skinny arms around his waist the way she often did when he was having feelings. "What'd you do to him?" she accused Jordan and Naomi.

"It's okay, sweetie," Adam managed. "They didn't do anything."

"Did he get emotional?" she asked knowingly.

"I suppose so," Jordan said.

Gus nodded sagely.

"You like my lights?" she asked brightly, accusations forgotten.

"They're great," the siblings chorused.

"They brought us some more," Adam said, holding them out to Gus.

"Thank you!" Gus said. She pointed to the house. "Wanna see them on?"

Adam watched Naomi's face turn hopeful for a split second, then politeness overtook hope.

"Oh, that's okay. We didn't want to intrude. Just snap a quick picture and drop these off."

"That's okay, right, Daddy?"

Adam smiled.

"Yeah, it's fine. You gonna do it?"

She grinned and ran for the side of the house. She'd become quite an expert at toggling the various power strips on over the last few weeks.

The house lit up and Naomi gasped. Adam hoped it was a happy gasp, although in his opinion the house was looking very overburdened: more light than structure.

"Wow," she said, and Jordan nodded. "It's beautiful."

Gus came skipping back to them, seemingly impervious to the cold.

"It's not the most lights *ever*," she said. "I looked it up. There's a family called the Gay family. Like you, Daddy. Anyway, they have way more, but theirs is a whole huge thing. But it's pretty good!"

Adam clamped his lips together and nodded.

"It looks amazing, honey," Naomi said. Then to Adam, "Do you mind if I take a picture?"

"Go for it. If you post it anywhere, though, will you not put our address? When I originally put out the call, I didn't think more than a few people would see it."

"Of course," she said. She took a few pictures, slid her phone in her pocket, and said, "I'll tag you." She was clearly stalling. Finally she turned to Gus and said, "You've got a great dad, you know?"

Gus grinned and nodded. "I know."

Adam saw Naomi's eyes fill with tears before she turned away. She and Jordan waved from the car as they drove off down Knockbridge Lane.

True to her word, a few hours later Naomi posted the picture with their address blurred out and tagged Adam. She wrote, *Nothing is as important as family. So lucky to see this labor of love by a father to make his daughter's dreams come true. #LitByLove.*

By the time he left work that day, Naomi's post had been shared enough times that Adam was getting follows and tags every few minutes. He couldn't wait to show Gus, who'd talked excitedly about Naomi and Jordan's visit the whole drive to school that morning.

When he turned onto Knockbridge Lane, something felt different. It looked brighter. For a moment, Adam thought it was all the lights on their house gleaming up the darkness. But as he rounded the bend, he saw the cars. Six or seven cars lined the street between their house and Wes', and people stood on the sidewalk, looking at the house, lights ablaze.

Adam parked in the driveway and got out, waving at them.

"Uh, hey, everyone."

A chorus of *Hey*s and *Sorry*s and *Awkward*s greeted him, and one woman approached him haltingly.

"This is super weird, probably, sorry," she said.

"It's okay. It's nice that people are interested," Adam said. "I'm surprised anyone would trek up here. Are you from around here?"

"My parents live down in Douglas and I'm visiting for Christmas." She shrugged. "Not much to do, so…"

Adam nodded. "I grew up here, so I know what you mean."

She grinned. "Cool if we take a picture?"

"It's fine. Just don't post my address if you share it, okay?"

"Sure thing, thanks. And Merry Christmas!" she called as he walked to the front door.

"Merry Christmas," Adam called back with a wave.

Adam was trying and failing to whistle "Joy to the World" as he walked in the door.

"I'm home!" he called to River and Gus, but it was Wes who stepped out of the kitchen.

"Hey," he said. "Hope you don't mind—"

Adam shut him up with a kiss to show him exactly how little he minded.

But whereas Wes usually wrapped his arms around Adam and kissed him deeply, now Wes was tense, his shoulders rigid.

"What's wrong?" Adam asked. "Is Gus okay? Where's River?"

Chapter Twenty-One

Wes

When Wes had seen the first car pull up while Gus was at school and Adam was at work, the first person get out to take a picture, he'd been mildly charmed. He knew Gus would get a kick out of it.

When the second car came, he felt his jaw clenching, teeth grinding.

When the third car came, his heart started to pound.

Through the window, he watched River and Gus get home, watched Gus flip the power strips on with glee. River took a selfie of them in front of the house, presumably to send to Adam, and they went inside.

When the fourth car came, Gus came outside and waved, and River peeked shyly through the window. Wes got the sense that River didn't appreciate the attention any more than Wes did, though likely for different reasons.

Gus went back inside, River pulled the curtains, and Knockbridge Lane went back to its usual sleepy quiet.

Wes relaxed. Some weirdos with nothing better to do than take pictures of Christmas lights wasn't a big deal. At least, that's what he told his clenched jaw, his grinding teeth, and his pounding heart. He stroked Bettie's back and recorded the results of his recent light readings as the sun set.

Then a camera flash bloomed in his periphery and Wes found himself sitting on the floor below window level, even though he was in the basement. He couldn't even be positive he'd *seen* the camera flash. But they were out there, just the way they used to be.

All Wes could think about then was Gus. He'd only been a little younger than her when he'd realized that his dad was famous. And a little older when he'd realized his dad wasn't nearly as famous as he wished he was. Gus might think this was fun at first—attention for a project that excited her.

But what about when she wanted to hang more lights and she and Adam couldn't go outside without people taking her picture and she didn't know how to get them to stop and she didn't want to be mean but she really, really needed to feel like a person instead of like something other people controlled like a puppet or a paper doll or a trading card and by then it was too late and she couldn't get out of it.

What about that?

Wes pulled on a hooded sweatshirt and heavy jacket and a hat and put the hood up over the hat and snuck out his own back door. He snuck down the road and around to the side of the Mills' house, and then walked to the front door with his back to the three people taking pictures.

Gus opened the door with a happy smile and pulled him inside.

"River, Wes is here!" she called happily.

River waved and then snuck a nervous glance outside.

"Those people still there?"

"Three of them."

"I wish this place had a back door," River muttered.

Wes fervently agreed.

They stood there awkwardly for a moment, River chewing their lip and Wes trying very hard to come up with a normal reason he'd come over that he could proffer to River. A reason that wasn't *I had a famous dad and I was famous for a second and it ruined my life and I'm FREAKING out right now.* Because River was Adam's sibling and he wanted to make a good impression.

"I, um, thought I could make dinner before Adam got home?"

It came out sounding like a choked question and River raised an eyebrow, but Gus looked up at him excitedly.

"What are you gonna make?"

Oops.

"Rice?" Wes offered, trying to think of the rest.

"Great. I love rice," Gus said.

She was such a damn gem.

"Okay," River said, clearly catching on that he didn't want to explain. "Maybe I'll take off if you're good to stay with her?"

"Sure."

"Okay, bye, Bug," they said, and hugged Gus.

They eyed the window.

"Here, do you want this?" Wes offered, pulling off his hooded sweatshirt.

River took it gratefully, though it was too big for them.

"Thank you," they said, pulled the hood up, and slipped out the door.

Wes opened the refrigerator and found some cauliflower and carrots that he cut up to stir-fry with the rice. He forced himself to focus only on making even, deliberate cuts, not on what might or might not be going on outside.

Gus chatted while he cooked, telling him about the words on her spelling test and how while red, blue, and yellow were the primary colors, light had its own primary colors, and it was red, blue, and green, did he know?

"And did you know," Gus went on fervently, "that there's no colors when you turn the lights off? They *disappear*! Where do they go? Nowhere! I don't know. No one knows where they go!"

Wes nodded and asked her more questions, but all the while he was thinking about that. He remembered learning it in elementary school—remembered a few people making much of it, existentially, in pondering (and ponderous) middle school poems.

But it was strange that Gus should bring it up now—the day before his father's birthday—because this was his father's problem. He felt like he disappeared when he didn't have the lights on him. And what Wes had chosen all those years ago, by stepping out of the spotlight himself, was to turn off a source of his father's light. His dad felt like Wes had made him disappear. And there was nothing he could do about that. No amount of explaining that he, Wes, felt like *he* disappeared when the lights were *on* him. It had never mattered, he realized, because his father didn't feel he disappeared any less for understanding it.

"Wes. Wes!" Gus was saying.

"Huh?"

"You look really weird. And the cauliflower is burning."

"Shit!"

Wes snatched the pan off the heat.

"Sorry, Gus."

She shrugged. "Why are you weird?"

"Oh, uh."

He knew about Adam and Gus' no lying policy and tried to figure out how to formulate an appropriate truth.

"Remember I told you I don't spend much time with my family?"

"Uh-huh."

"Tomorrow is my dad's birthday, so he's been on my mind. And thinking about stuff with him makes me kind of…stressed-out."

"Oh. Like Daddy feels about money?"

Wes filed that tidbit away.

"Probably something like that, yeah."

He didn't feel the need to disclose that her lights were currently driving him to near panic attack levels of anxiety. One truth was probably enough.

"You could send him an e-card," Gus suggested.

"Oh, yeah?" Wes said absently.

"Yeah. Daddy says that's what you do when you don't really care about someone but you have to keep up appearances." She shrugged. "Appearances of what?"

Wes snorted with amusement and decided then and there never to say anything in front of Gus that he wouldn't want repeated in the worst possible context.

"Thanks for the suggestion."

Wes scraped rice and slightly burned stir-fry into a bowl and put it on the kitchen table. It didn't look very appetizing, but Gus seemed game.

"Daddy will be home in a minute. We should wait for him because of politeness."

Wes high-fived her as the front door opened and Adam arrived.

"Gus is fine," Wes assured Adam. "And River left because I came over. I, uh, made dinner. Kind of."

"Daddy!" Gus threw herself at him. "Wes made rice!"

"Thanks," Adam said, looking at him questioningly. "I'm happy to see you."

"Me too," Wes said. "You too, I mean."

He couldn't quite get himself together. He knew he was behaving strangely but he had that feeling. The feeling he hadn't had much since meeting Adam, but had apparently only lain dormant. The sense of being inside his prison of a body as one by one his limbs began to feel strange and alien.

But Adam just smiled at him and followed Gus back into the kitchen.

Wes forced his prison to walk into the kitchen and get bowls out of the cabinet. He made it scoop rice and vegetables into the bowls. He made it say *Thanks* when Adam got out silverware and asked if he wanted water. He made it bend its legs and sit down at the table and scoop food into its untasting mouth. He made it nod when people talked and made it smile when they smiled.

And all the while, he felt flashbulbs going off in his face as he shrank smaller and smaller inside his panopticon.

After dinner, Adam asked him to stay, but Wes knew that he couldn't keep up the charade once they were one-on-one. And he didn't want the alien prison to touch Adam. It felt like watching someone else touch him.

"Sorry, I can't. I'm…"

"Your dad's birthday's tomorrow, right?" Adam said, knowingly.

"Yeah."

Wes was touched he'd remembered. At least, he would be if he could feel anything except disgust for the prison and the people who looked at it.

"I understand," Adam said. But he didn't, because Wes couldn't tell him. Not right now.

Wes pulled Adam close to the prison, wishing his warmth could penetrate its walls.

"Talk tomorrow, okay?" Adam said, and Wes nod-ded, desperate to get home so he could sort himself out. He'd text Adam later and apologize for not being as affectionate as he wanted to be. For being strange.

He pulled on his coat and hat, only remembering he'd given his hoodie to River as he closed the front door behind him.

And someone shoved a news camera directly in his face.

Chapter Twenty-Two

Adam

Adam heard indistinct voices outside as he cleaned up the dinner dishes, but paid them no mind until someone shouted. Then, curious, he poked his head out the front door. A woman with a microphone was standing on his driveway speaking into a camera. Was it…the news?

"What the hell?" Adam muttered, stepping into his boots.

"Adam Mills?" the woman said when she saw him.

"Uh, yeah?"

"I'm Tamara Michaelson and we're filming for KCWY. I'd love to interview you about your lights! We're doing feel-good pieces to intro and close out each news broadcast, and the story of your lights is just the thing for us. I tried to call you, but your number isn't listed."

She was blinking at him brightly.

"Oh, um, wow," Adam said. "I can't believe you think this is newsworthy."

"A parent's love for their child is just the kind of *up* story our viewers will love," Tamara Michaelson said.

"Well, sure, then. Cool."

Adam was just sorry Gus had gone to bed already, because she would love this.

"Daddy!" a familiar voice hissed from the front door.

And there was Gus, in pajamas, boots, and a hat, looking excited and guilty.

"Can I please come see?"

Adam smiled and gestured her outside. She'd be a grouch in the morning, but it was the last day of school before vacation anyway.

"Yay!"

She pulled her coat on as she came.

"You must be Gus," Tamara Michaelson said with a smile. "Want to be on TV? If it's all right with your dad, that is."

It's your funeral, Adam thought, but said, "It's fine with me."

Tamara Michaelson and the camera operator set up the shot of the house lit up sky-high, Adam and Gus in front of it. Gus was vibrating with excitement.

"Do you think Wes sees us?" Gus asked, waving at his house.

"I'm in Garnet Run, standing in front of a labor of love. Adam Mills and his daughter, Gus, have been collecting lights to decorate their house all month, and a recent outpouring of support on Instagram has made it a sight to behold. Mr. Mills, can you tell us how this began?"

"Well, I asked Gus what would make her happy this year, and she said she wanted a lot of lights, so—"

"The *most* lights," Gus corrected. "I wanted the most lights *ever*."

"It looks like you've got them!" Tamara Michaelson said cheerily.

"No," said Gus. "I looked it up. The most is by the Gay family, in New York." Tamara Michaelson opened her mouth, but Gus continued. "Daddy wanted me to be happy because we had to move and I was sad."

"Why did you have to move, sweetie?" Michaelson asked, clearly hoping for some viral video tale of a holiday miracle.

"Papa didn't want to be my dad anymore, so Daddy brought us back here, and said we'd have the best time on our own. But we're not on our own anymore," Gus rambled.

"That's right," Michaelson said, trying to regain control of her interview. "You have a lot of people who want to help you."

Gus shook her head. Adam knew what she was about to say: that they had Wes now. But Adam cut her off.

"That's right," he said. "I want to thank everyone who sent or dropped off lights. It was so generous of you, and Gus and I really appreciate it. Right, sweetie?"

"Right!"

Michaelson nodded at him gratefully and turned back to the camera.

"There you have it," she said, voice fixed precisely in human interest timbre. "A community's generosity can make all the difference in a family's life. Good night, and happy holidays."

She turned back to Adam and Gus and held out her hand. Gus shook it, then Adam.

"Thank you," she said. "That was great."

"I hope you can edit," Adam muttered.

She winked at him and gave a warm smile.

"Not necessary."

Back inside, Adam attempted to get Gus back to bed, but she was so hyped up that it took an hour to calm her down. When he'd finally turned out her light, leaving her in the soft glow of her kale plant, Adam collapsed on the sofa, flicked on the TV fire, and took out his phone to fill Wes in on the excitement, in case he hadn't seen it from his window.

A tiny warmth kindled in his stomach when he saw he already had a text from Wes. He opened it excitedly, then his stomach seized.

Wes: I can't do this. I'm sorry. We have to be done.

"Wait," Adam said to no one. "What?"

He read it again because clearly he was missing something.

But no. That's all the text said.

Adam called Wes but he didn't answer.

"What the hell."

He texted: You can't just text me that and then not answer the phone, Wes. PLEASE pick up. Gus is asleep and I can't leave.

He waited a minute, then called again. This time, Wes answered. His voice sounded strange and croaky.

"I'm sorry," he said.

"What's going on? Are you okay? I don't understand. What do you mean we're done?"

Adam could feel the tears flooding his eyes and knew that soon his voice would sound squeaky and emotional. He'd come to terms with being an emotional person a long time ago, but he still resented that when he got angry he cried.

"I'm so sorry," Wes said again. "I just can't. I thought I could be... I thought with you I could... But I just can't. It's too much. I'm... God, I'm so sorry."

Then he hung up.

Furious, Adam called him right back. He picked up but didn't speak.

"Wes, come on. What happened? You can't... We had... What the hell is going on?"

Wes sighed and when he spoke again his voice was choked. Desperate.

"Please," he said. "Please just leave me alone."

The line went dead and Adam let the phone slide from suddenly numb fingers.

Outside, the lights still lit the night cheerily. The fire still crackled merrily on the television. Gus still slumbered sweetly in her bed.

But everything was different now.

Adam was alone again. And this time he didn't even know why.

Chapter Twenty-Three

Adam

Adam woke on the couch, fire still blazing on the TV, neck crooked painfully, with Gus standing over him.

"Can I have waffles with faces?" she asked excitedly, then crowed, "It's almost vacation!"

Adam's eyelids felt like they were made of sand, and his mouth tasted like he'd licked stamps in hell. When he managed to sit up, his skull protested by splitting in two and running in opposite directions away from his cringing brain.

Oh, right. The wine.

After Wes had destroyed him with sentence fragments like shrapnel he'd opened a bottle and attempted to play Sherlock Holmes with his life.

With a physical form that made him long for death and nary a clue to show for his investigations, Adam concluded that there was a reason Sherlock was more into cocaine than white wine.

"Um," he said intelligently.

"Great!" Gus said, and skipped into the kitchen in her red-and-white-striped pajamas, like the world's loudest candy cane.

Adam disagreed with the word on principle at the moment, but if there was one thing he would not do it was ruin Gus' mood with his own heartbreak. There'd be time enough for that later, unfortunately.

So he scraped himself off the couch, instructed his emotions to stay coiled acidly in his stomach, and dragged himself into the kitchen to slice strawberries and arrange them in smiling faces on his daughter's morning waffles.

Work was a nightmare. Adam was not good at keeping his emotions inside. Even customers so oblivious they asked where the hammers were while standing in front of the hammers asked Adam what was wrong. When Marie told him his "Nothing!"'s were scaring the customers he switched to, "Oh, just a bad day. Now what can I help you with?"

But it was a losing battle. By the time he left work early to pick up Gus—something he'd planned weeks ago to celebrate the start of her vacation—his eyes were red with unshed (and some shed-in-the-bathroom) tears and his lips bitten red.

He knew what he really needed was a couple of days on his own to cry his heart out and watch old movies while he ate cookie dough from the tube, but he didn't have that luxury.

Instead, he blasted Christmas music on the radio, rolled the windows down, and scream-sang along at the top of his lungs as the freezing wind reddened his whole face to match his eyes. There was a kind of exultant frenzy to it that made Adam feel better enough that he arrived at Gus' school in a state that could easily be misread as pre-vacation sugar high mania, rather than heartbroken despair.

So that was good.

Gus ran to the car with her arms full of papers and her scarf streaming behind her, and immediately began to chatter excitedly about a science project she wanted to talk to Wes about.

That…wasn't.

Adam and Gus lay on the couch, legs interlaced, staring blankly at the marathon of old Christmas movies on TV.

Gus had taken the news that Wes wouldn't be spending Christmas with them hard. At first, she'd asked if he decided to go visit his parents after all, and Adam had dearly wanted to say yes and avoid the entire conversation. Have their Christmas and hide his feelings from Gus until after. But that would only delay the inevitable. Besides, he was terrible at hiding his feelings.

And, most importantly: no lying.

So he'd told her the truth, as gently as he could, and then he'd taken his emotions to the shower and cried them out under a fall of water so hot it was almost painful.

Not as painful as the truth, though.

That this was precisely what Adam had been trying to avoid: bringing another adult into Gus' life that she admired—no, *loved*—and that person abandoning her. He cursed himself for bringing this pain into Gus' life.

But when the water started to lose heat, so did his temper, and he wept a gentler kind of tears—these for himself. Because the truth was that he'd fallen in love with a kind, brilliant, sweet, gorgeous, weird man whom he'd thought might love him too. Might love Gus. Might want to make a family with them.

And he'd been wrong.

So wrong.

The worst kind of wrong. The kind that sucker punched the breath from your lungs and left only emptiness in its place.

Adam had to work the next day and River had been going to hang out with Gus, but Gus was feeling tender and begged to come to work with him instead. She promised that she wouldn't be any trouble and that she'd read in the back, so Adam texted Charlie and got his okay.

It was three days till Christmas.

Gus had cheered a little at the rare opportunity to hang out in Matheson's, but as they pulled out of the driveway, both their eyes went to Wes' house.

The paper, which had come down window by window over the last weeks, almost without Adam's notice, was back, and the whole place had an air of remoteness about it once more.

Adam realized that once he got to know Wes he'd stopped thinking of his house as creepy or sad. It was just the place where Wes did his experiments and had his brilliant ideas. The home of Wes' unusual menagerie that Gus loved.

That Wes hadn't cared about keeping up the landscaping or the exterior paint made sense—he just had other things he cared about.

Unfortunately, Adam wasn't one of them anymore.

The pain hit again and Adam cringed in the driver's seat.

Gus fell silent and fidgeted with the fringe on her scarf.

As they turned onto the main road, snow falling softly, the snowy mountains in the distance glowing against the blue sky, Gus said, "It's the lights."

"What's the lights, sweetie?"

"The lights made Wes go away."

Something more delicate than pain clawed at Adam's guts and he pulled the car over to the side of the road and faced his daughter.

"Baby, no."

"I wanted the most lights to have fun without Papa, and that's what made Wes help us, and then when we got a lot, it made him leave."

Her lip was trembling, and Adam realized that this was what she'd been holding on to since he told her: guilt.

"Listen to me, Gus. Wes didn't leave because of the lights, or anything else because of you. Wes thinks you're great. In fact, we got to know Wes because he thought you were so cool and smart and interesting."

Slash because you broke into his house, Adam added to himself, knowing someday they'd laugh about that. About the time Adam dated the neighbor for a few months because Gus pulled a B&E.

Gus sniffed miserably.

"I think they're magic," she said, like she hadn't heard him at all.

"I didn't think you believed in magic," Adam said gently.

She shook her head and when she looked back up at him it was with his sister's eyes. Eyes far too old for an eight-year-old.

"Maybe you don't have to believe in things for them to be real," she said in a haunted voice. "Just like sometimes you can believe things really a lot, and they never become real."

This was the saddest thing he'd ever heard Gus say.

"Is there something you believed in a lot that didn't become real?" he forced himself to say, dreading her answer.

But Gus just looked at him with those ancient eyes and said, "Never mind, Dad."

She'd never called him Dad before.

True to her word, Gus read in Charlie's office the whole morning. At lunchtime, Charlie showed up with a stack of pizzas for everyone in the store. The waft of hot cheese lured Gus out, and they enjoyed a pleasant hour eating and chatting.

As the pizza boxes were cleared away, Gus turned big eyes on Charlie and said, "Can I please have a job?"

For a moment, Charlie's eyes got as big as Gus' and Adam could see him working out how to let her down easy by citing child labor laws.

"I think she means a job to do for the afternoon," Adam murmured.

"Oh." Charlie looked relieved. "Sure thing. Let me introduce you to the different sizes of nails."

Gus' eyes lit up and she followed Charlie eagerly.

"Thanks, Charlie," Adam said when he returned, Gus happily sorting the bins of nails and humming along with Christmas carols on the radio. "Um. Wes broke up with me. Us. Me."

Charlie frowned, his red-brown eyebrows drawing together.

"I'm real sorry, Adam. That's a hell of a thing to deal with at the holidays." He glanced over at Gus. "Does she know?"

"Yeah. It's been a crappy couple days. That's why I didn't want to leave her alone today. Thanks for letting her come in. I—"

"Shh, don't worry about it," Charlie said, putting a large, warm hand on Adam's shoulder.

A customer approached and Adam rang him up while Charlie inquired after his family.

"Do you know why?" Charlie asked when they'd left.

Adam shook his head.

"He just said he couldn't do it. He thought he could, but he was wrong. And he asked me to leave him alone."

"Huh."

He looked contemplative.

"Huh, what?"

"Well, I know I'm not exactly in the know here, but that sounds like someone who's scared."

"Scared of what?"

Charlie shook his head, expression serious.

"I don't know."

At 3:00 p.m., Charlie flipped the sign on the door to *Closed* and told them all to get out of there. Gus made them all wait another five minutes until she'd perfectly sorted the last nail into its proper container, then collapsed dramatically on the floor, sniffing her metallic fingertips and making Vanna White-esque arm gestures to show off her work.

"Good job," Charlie said. "Come back in ten years and I'll give you a job."

Gus nodded seriously and Adam smiled.

As they trouped out into the parking lot, Charlie pressed an envelope into Adam's hand.

"Merry Christmas," he said.

Adam's face must've expressed his panic at not having anything for Charlie, because the big man chuckled and said, "Holiday bonus. You deserve it."

Then he loped off to his truck, calling, "Have a good one," behind him.

Adam peeked into the envelope and saw a check for five hundred dollars.

"Holy shit," Adam murmured.

"What's that?" Gus asked, skipping up to him.

"Oh, um, Charlie gave me a holiday bonus."

"Like, money?"

"Yeah." Adam chucked her under the chin, smiling. "Like, money."

The snow had stopped falling and it was a beautiful, clear day despite the cold.

"Hey, you wanna go visit River at the cat shelter?"

"Yeah!"

Gus ran to the car and Adam shot River a quick text, and got their enthusiastic response immediately.

On the way, they stopped at Peach's Diner, which had been in Garnet Run as long as Adam could remember, and picked up a pie.

The Dirt Road Cat Shelter looked cheery, with purple, white, and yellow lights in every window.

"Love the color scheme," Adam said.

"Thanks." River smiled. "Rye let me do the decorations."

"River, River, can I do one?"

Gus was standing at the front desk, where crayon drawings of cats who'd been adopted were taped.

"Sure, Bug."

River sat Gus on the chair and set her up with paper and crayons. Adam unboxed the apple pie and they ate it with spoons right from the tin.

Adam had told River about Wes via text that morning in explaining why he was taking Gus to work with him, and Adam could tell River had a million questions.

"You okay here for a minute, sweetie?" Adam said. "I wanna cuddle some cats."

Gus nodded, totally focused on her drawing, and Adam and River went into the large cat playroom.

Adam felt instantly calmed by the cats snoozing on perches and curled up in corners around the room. Two played with something that looked like a felt Pop-Tart on the floor, rolling around together and coming to rest in a single floof of fur and paws, looking up at River.

"Hi, Dancer, hi, Prancer," River said. "Just temporary names," they muttered. "So what the hell happened with Wes?"

River picked up either Dancer or Prancer, cuddling the tabby cat to their chest where it settled and began to purr loudly.

"Uggh." Adam scrubbed his hands over his face. "That's what's killing me. I don't know."

"He seemed pretty tense when he showed up the other day. When all the people were taking pictures. I was too." River kissed the cat between its ears. "He gave me his hoodie when I went to leave, so I could cover my face."

Somehow, despite all its abuse, Adam's heart still soared. That was so kind. So like Wes.

"He did?"

"Yeah. He seemed… I don't know. Spooked, maybe? Is he in witness protection or something?"

"I wish," Adam muttered. Then, realizing how horrible that was, said. "God, no, I don't wish that. I just meant that I wish he had a good reason for breaking up with me."

"What would be a good reason?" River asked curiously.

"I dunno. Like, we fought all the time, or I cheated on him, or, or, or I stole all his money or something."

River looked doubtful.

"You would never do those things."

"I know, I just mean a real reason."

River bit their lip.

"Those just sound like easy reasons. Clear reasons. But I think sometimes it's more likely that the reasons are complicated…subtle."

River's eyes had taken on a faraway look and Adam wondered if they'd been dating someone.

"Anyway, I just think sometimes it's not quite so clear-cut," River concluded. "And by the way, you probably wouldn't know if he was in witness protection. I mean, that's kind of the whole idea."

They said it casually, and half-joking, but it made Adam realize that he actually didn't know that much about Wes. So much of the time they'd spent together had focused on what Adam and Gus needed—hanging the lights, show-and-tell, estate sales, Gus' interest in Wes' critters. And when they'd talked about Wes, it had mostly been about his research and experiments.

Most of what Adam knew about Wes came from observing his behavior. Adam knew he was kind and generous and patient because he'd seen him be all those things. And, of course, funny and smart and hot as hell.

In fact, most of what Adam knew about Wes' past was about the unfortunate experience he'd had with acting and his father.

…And how he absolutely hated attention. The kind of attention that Adam's Instagram posts had brought down on the street.

Oh, no.

Chapter Twenty-Four

Wes

Wes hadn't slept since ending things with Adam.

Since the night before the strangers with their phones and the newscaster with her camera had shattered his conviction that he could be a normal person living a normal life with another person in the world.

He'd plastered the windows with paper and locked the door, and it had still taken hours for him to stop shaking; to realize that the cameras hadn't been there for him. And that likely they wouldn't be back.

With realization came despair.

First it was *What the hell have I done*. Then, when he'd calmed down a bit, it was *How do I fix this*. In that mode, he'd picked up his phone a dozen times, fingers hovering over messages to Adam that said *NEVER MIND I JUST PANICKED I AM SO DAMN SORRY!* Then, seeing the messages he actually had sent to Adam, he'd cringed and moved on to *They're better off without me*. Swift on its heels: *God, I miss them*.

Finally, rage. Rage at himself for still not being over this reaction. Then rage at his father for all of it. By that time, it was the next day—his father's birthday—and Wes picked up and put down his phone all over again.

Janice and Banana had been very happy to have him awake the night before, back to their nocturnal schedule, and had gamboled around, scratching at the piles he'd made for them in their enclosure. But come morning, when they'd crashed, Wes hadn't gone to bed.

And now, hours later, he picked up his phone one more time, and this time, he dialed.

His father answered in the hearty, hail-fellow-well-met voice he used for journalists, producers, and now, it seemed, his son.

"Happy birthday," Wes said, because his mind went blank of every other thing he wanted to say.

"Well, thank you. I'm surprised to hear from you."

"Yeah."

An awkward silence during which Wes could hear the jazzy Christmas music his parents had played during December since he was a child.

Wes walked to the periscope and looked at Adam and Gus' house. The lights were off and all he could see was the flicker that meant the TV was on in the living room. He wondered if Gus' kale plant was still glowing or if the luciferase had worn off.

He wondered what Gus and Adam were watching. He wondered if Adam had told Gus he wouldn't be around anymore.

He wondered a lot of things he'd probably never know the answers to. Not as long as his only access to them was through this damned periscope.

Adam's voice on the phone had been so hurt and confused. Shocked.

"Westley, are you there?" came his father's oil-slick voice.

Wes intended to say, "What are you doing for your birthday this year." But what came out instead was quite different.

"You weren't a very good father."

"Excuse me?" Nigel Brennan said, voice now cold as ice.

It was the voice the public never heard—except for the brief arc where he'd played his own evil twin on *Edge of Day*. That voice had made Wes shudder when his father slid into it in response to Wes' revelation that he was done with show business and it made him shudder now.

He kept his eyes fixed on Adam and Gus' house through the periscope, remembered how it had felt to be up on their roof, with the big sky around him and the cold wind nipping at his ears. When he'd hung lights, he hadn't worried about the neighbors seeing him because he'd been focused on making Gus and Adam happy. He remembered how it felt to speak to Gus' classmates about Bettie. Though he'd been nervous at first, he hadn't worried about them looking at him because none of them found him even one-tenth as interesting as his tarantula.

The newscaster had scared him. Terrified him, in fact. But even she had only cared about what he might have to say about Adam and Gus' lights.

It was the wound of trauma that was reopened

every time someone paid overt attention to him. Now
the wound could open at a hair trigger, and those trig-
gers had become phobias. He knew it. He just wasn't
quite sure what to do about it.

But he *did* know what to do about his father's dis-
approving, judgmental, entitled voice.

"You heard me. I didn't know any different at the
time. But I know now what it looks like to be a good
father. You model best practices for your children.
You show them how to make the world a better, more
interesting, more loving place. You're honest with
them because trust between you matters. You ask
them how they feel and why they feel it and you honor
those feelings. You don't instrumentalize them for
your own gain. And you don't ever, *ever* make them
feel responsible for your happiness as a person."

Wes could hear the cold fury in his voice so he
knew his father could hear it too.

"I was so terrified of hurting you, of ruining your
career, that I did things I hated. Things that hurt me.
That are still hurting me now. And you didn't care.
You didn't care how I felt or what I needed. You only
cared about yourself. I know that now. And I know
how selfish that is."

Wes took a deep breath. He felt as if a huge weight
had slid off his shoulders, and his heart was pounding with adrenaline.

"I'm sorry to say this on your birthday, but I can't
sit with it for one more day. I did something that hurt
people I care about yesterday because I was so terrified of being visible in the world. It was a stupid

mistake and I regret it, but I don't know if I can ever make it right. But I'm sure as hell gonna try."

He wasn't even talking to his father anymore. He was just saying aloud the things that needed to be said.

Before his father could say anything in response, Wes blurted out, "Happy birthday," and hung up the phone.

He was shaking.

"Holy shit," Wes said. "Holy, holy, holy shit."

He slid down to the floor, back against the wall. His hands were trembling but he felt exultant, like he'd finally beaten an enemy in a game he hadn't even admitted he was playing.

And if he could do that...if he could face his father after all these years and tell him exactly what he thought of him?

Then he could do anything.

He grabbed a piece of cardboard lying near him and a marker near his foot and started to make a plan. He sketched and calculated and plotted and schemed.

Then he picked up his phone and placed one more call.

"Zachary?" he said when his friend picked up. "I'm sorry to bother you, but I need you to help me save Christmas."

Chapter Twenty-Five

Adam

It was the day before Christmas Eve and Adam and Gus were trying to pretend like they were having fun. It was a rather pitiful scene.

Adam kept coming back to his realization about Wes and what might have gone wrong between them, and why. He'd composed and deleted three separate text messages, because if he was wrong…well, it felt too pathetic to text the guy who broke up with you and say, "I think I figured out why you dumped me and I'm sorry and here's how we can fix it" and have him say, "No, actually, I dumped you because I'm just not that into you."

Adam cringed and sternly banished the thought, resolving yet again to be present with Gus. His heartbreak would still be there after Christmas was over.

"Hey, I know," Adam said. "Let's go get a Christmas tree!"

Gus lifted her drooping head at that idea, but then slumped back onto the couch.

"I don't wanna murder a tree," she said.

"We could get a fake tree," Adam offered, but even

as he was saying it he worried they'd be sold out at the few nearby stores.

Gus just sighed and flipped over on the couch so her blond hair streamed to the floor.

Adam tapped around on his phone, then went to sit beside her.

"Look, here. We could get a tree that has the root ball still attached and that way we can plant it again after Christmas."

Gus sat up.

"We don't have any ornaments," she said, but he could tell her interest was piqued.

"We can make them!"

"Hmm." Gus contemplated for a minute, then jumped up. "Okay!"

Adam grabbed her in a hug. She was truly the greatest kid on the planet.

"Thanks for being a sport," he said. "I'm sorry this Christmas hasn't turned out as good as I promised."

"It's not your fault," she sighed.

It was, but Adam chose to accept her absolution in the spirit in which it was given.

The Christmas tree farm was about thirty minutes away and they sang along to Christmas carols the whole way, moods lifting with each mile they got from home. It was good to just *leave* sometimes, Adam realized. To physically distance yourself from your problems so you could get some perspective. It had certainly worked with Mason. Mostly.

"Why's it called a carol?" Gus mused.

"I have no idea. Look it up."

He passed her his phone.

She read, "Middle English, ring, circle of stones, enclosed place for study (see carrel), ring dance with song (hence, song)." Then she trailed off and said, "Do you speak Latin?"

"I don't think anyone really speaks Latin anymore."

"Oh. It says something in Latin and then 'piper for dance.'"

"Cool. So the word for the circle of stones that they danced in became the word for the song."

"Words are neat," Gus said, handing back the phone.

"Have I told you lately that you're the greatest kid in the known universe?"

She grinned. "Nope."

"Well. You're the greatest kid in the known universe."

"What about the unknown universe?"

"I can't be sure. But you're probably the greatest kid there too."

At the farm, they parked in the cordoned-off area and got out to peruse.

"Hey, there," said a man who looked almost comically like a lumberjack. Although Adam supposed if there were any place it was reasonable to find a lumberjack it was around trees. "A last-minute shopper."

"Yeah." Adam snugged his hat down over his ears. "Life, you know?" he said by way of explanation.

The bearded man nodded.

"I do. So what kind of tree can we match you up with?"

"We need one that won't die," Gus said.

"Ah, got it. I have just the thing."

They followed the man's broad, flannel-clad form down a row of trees to ones that were in tubs.

"These have their root balls wrapped in burlap. You can plant them as soon as the ground thaws and until then keep them alive by watering them in the tub."

Gus gave a nod to indicate these trees passed muster, and she went to look around while Adam paid.

"Uh, any chance you know how to attach this tree to my car?" Adam asked, and the lumberjack clapped him on the back and went to get the rope.

"How far you goin?" he asked.

"To Garnet Run."

"Sorry, I'm not familiar. I just moved here last month."

"Oh, where from?"

"Olympia, Washington."

Adam nodded. "Garnet Run's about half an hour away. It's small. No reason you'd know it. Are you living around here?"

"Yeah, I've been subletting from the guy who owns this place while I work it for him. But the job ends—well, now, really. He'll be out of town till summer, and then I'll find another place. I'm Bram, by the way." He held out his hand.

"Adam. Nice to meet you. That's my daughter, Gus."

"She likes trees, huh?"

"Yeah, she said she didn't want to murder a tree for Christmas."

Bram smiled. Although he was quite a large man, he had a free, easy smile.

"I happen to agree with her."

Adam forced himself not to say, *But clearly you fell trees for a living.*

Bram laughed.

"You must be a terrible poker player, cuz I can tell exactly what you're thinking."

Adam flushed, but Bram didn't seem the slightest bit bothered.

"Yeah, well."

"Anyway, let's get this puppy strapped on."

Adam watched as Bram lifted the tree onto the top of his car and secured it. He handed Adam the bucket it came in and took his money with another easy smile.

"Time to go, Gus," Adam called, and she came running, the tip of her nose pink from the cold.

"What was the name of that town, again?" Bram asked.

"Garnet Run."

"Thanks," he said. "I'll get the lay of the land soon enough."

"Thank you," Adam and Gus chorused as they got into the car.

What a nice man, Adam thought. If only he weren't totally smitten with another.

They spent a surprisingly pleasant day making ornaments for the tree and watching the cheesiest romantic comedies they could find. Gus had the idea that they could take some of the bits of metal she'd gotten at the estate sale and repurpose them into ornaments, which is how they ended the day regarding with satisfaction a Christmas tree bedecked with glittered toilet paper roll snowflakes and hunks of metal hung with paper clips.

"They really shine," Adam said of the hunks of metal.

He lifted Gus up so she could place the tree topper, a paper towel roll snowflake covered in red glitter.

They'd snagged a few strings of lights from the side of the house to light the tree. Gus hadn't wanted to turn them on anymore anyway. So now the tree twinkled happily in the corner of the living room.

They ate mac and cheese and leftover Christmas monster cookies in front of *Home Alone*. Gus had never seen it and was overjoyed that there was a tarantula in it. Adam had forgotten about the tarantula and was decidedly underjoyed to see it.

Gus was nodding off before the movie ended, so Adam shut off the TV and the tree lights, and they brushed their teeth and went to bed.

It wasn't the most festive night, but it had definitely ended better than it had begun, so Adam considered it a win.

They spent the day of Christmas Eve sledding down the hill behind The Dirt Road Cat Shelter with River. Midmorning, Charlie and Rye, and Charlie's brother, Jack, and Jack's partner, Simon, showed up and joined them, as did one of River's friends, Tracy.

Adam hadn't been particularly looking forward to a day of sledding—cold and wet and sweaty was not his favorite combination—but it was what Gus had wanted to do, and River had arranged it. It had turned out to be a blast, however. As fun as the actual sledding was, Adam was having an even better time watching a gaggle of grownups attempting to fit on sleds clearly made for children.

Charlie and Rye were especially amusing because Charlie's muscular bulk meant that the sled didn't want to move, so Rye was having him push the sled and then jump on before it crested the hill, leading to several unexpected accelerations and one notable instance when Charlie missed the sled altogether, and Rye rocketed down the hill by himself while Charlie rolled down, ass over elbow for a few feet, then came to an undignified stop in the snow.

They all loved Gus and she was having the time of her life being the center of their attention (not to mention having their assistance carrying her sled back up the hill).

As the sun began to set and the warmth of home and hearth—or in Adam and Gus' case, home and TV fire—beckoned, they went their separate ways.

"We'll see you tomorrow, around eleven?" Adam asked River.

They nodded, cheeks flushed with cold, smiling. "Can't wait." They winked at Adam, indicating that everything was set on their end for Gus' gift.

"Bye, River!" Gus called. Then she practically collapsed into the car, lips chapped, eyes bright, and hair everywhere.

"Have fun, baby?" Adam asked.

"So much fun!"

"Good! What should we do tonight?"

Her smile faded. Adam knew what she was thinking. That they'd planned to spend the evening with Wes.

"Maybe we should try baking more Christmas cookies," Adam suggested brightly, wanting to preserve her previous good mood.

"Maybe," she murmured.

When they turned the corner onto Knockbridge Lane, the first thing Adam saw were the lights. For a moment, he didn't think anything of it—after all, besides the last two days, they'd had the house lit up at night since they'd started collecting lights.

But this wasn't just fairy lights. This was…

"Oh my god," Gus breathed in awe. "The lights are magic."

Their house and the trees and the lawn around it were…glowing.

It was a green familiar to everyone on Knockbridge Lane because every night it emanated from Wes Mobray's basement windows. A green that had led Marcy Pennywhistle and her sister to the conviction that Wes Mobray was a sorcerer.

But no one—Adam included—would ever be able to think of that green as evil again. Because now it was the glowing green of pine trees, holly leaves, and wreaths.

The green of Christmas.

It truly did look magical. Adam stopped the car at the curb to take it all in.

There were more fairy lights filling in the sides of the house where they'd run out. The windows each seemed aglow with candle lights, and the ground sparkled with a net of twinkles, like stars had fallen to earth.

The three large trees in the front and side of the house glowed with a subtle pulsation, just like the trees they'd seen in the clearing in the woods with Wes. On the front door was a large wreath that seemed to be made of antlers woven with boughs of holly.

But although he agreed with Gus that the glowing lights *looked* magic, it was something else entirely that held all the magic for Adam.

Across the front of the house, five words glowed in bioluminescent light: *I love you. I'm sorry.*

And there, on the front step of their house, in full view of all Knockbridge Lane, bundled up against the Wyoming December, sat Wes Mobray.

Chapter Twenty-Six

Wes

When Adam's car had pulled out of the driveway that morning, Wes and Zachary had sprung into action, implementing the plan Wes had spent the night crafting. And bless Zachary for acting like it was no big deal for Wes to call him in a frenzy and request a visit when they'd never met in person before. When he'd opened the door, Zachary had just smiled and said, "My friend." And Wes had known he truly was.

The real trick was controlling the form of the bioluminescence. That and the cold. Zachary had brought some tricks of the trade from his cache of Halloween decorations to help with both.

Wes had taken a deep breath, set his jaw, and walked across the street to the Mills' house in broad daylight, without Adam and Gus there as a buffer.

The guy with the gaggle of yappy poodles walked by, dogs booted and jacketed in different colors. Wes stood very still, as if he could disappear. But the man just walked by.

Mrs. Whatshername from next door came out to get the mail, shielded her eyes from the sun, and peered over. But she just gave an awkward little salute, as if the sight of two grown men with armfuls of lights, wires, and glowing bioluminescent material was perfectly normal. Wes supposed that after the time Adam and Gus had spent lighting their house up, it kind of was.

As they worked, Wes composed a speech. The speech he would give to Adam when he got home. It was full of heartfelt confessions, fears, and promises. It was full of explanations and plans.

But when Adam's car turned the corner of Knockbridge Lane, Wes forgot every single word he'd rehearsed. The only word he could remember was *home*. Because that's what Adam felt like to him.

Adam's lips formed his name and Gus ran to the middle of the yard to get the full effect of the lights. Wes tried to wave but his body seemed to have stiffened up as he sat on the stoop. He wasn't sure how long he'd been there, but he'd watched the dark set in.

Adam approached him slowly, eyes darting warily from him to Gus to the house that screamed the five words Wes wanted to say.

Usually, Adam was so full of emotion that it practically leaked from him. But now, he was oddly calm. He regarded Wes for a minute, then said, "Come in. You must be freezing."

Wes staggered to his feet. Still the words wouldn't come.

He lurched inside and fumbled his jacket and boots off. Adam guided him into the living room and into the easy chair, and before he knew it, he was swaddled in a blanket and Adam and Gus were staring at him from the couch—twin blond, blue-eyed angels waiting for him to speak.

Once, his fourth year of graduate school, Wes had stayed in the lab for the whole weekend working on an experiment. When someone entered on Monday morning and asked him a question, Wes had opened his mouth to answer and found words utterly inaccessible.

That was how he felt now. He cleared his throat to buy time and Adam's uncanny calm cracked.

"Are you okay?" he asked, leaning forward. "Do you mean what you wrote on the house? What happened?"

Under the warmth of Adam's care, Wes thawed and felt things begin to work again.

"I'm so sorry," he said. "I panicked and I couldn't explain, but I'm ready to talk now. And…yes." His heart flickered back to life. "I meant it. Completely."

Adam's blue eyes were usually the blue of the sky in a painting of a rural idyll. Now they glowed with a hot longing that warmed Wes deep inside. He wanted to grab Adam to him, pull him into the bed, wrap him in his body and explain everything under the cover of proximate flesh.

Adam, he saw now, would always listen to what he had to say.

But Adam wasn't the one who spoke next.

Gus stood, squared her narrow shoulders, and looked at Wes with the seriousness of someone who knows what it is to lose people.

"I'm so mad at you," she said. "You can't be our friend one day and then be mean to us the next. That's *not* being a good friend. Right?" she asked Adam.

"That's true, sweetie," Adam said, and Wes could tell that was something Adam had told her, likely about a friend of hers.

"You made me and Daddy really sad," Gus went on. "We were very nice to you and you were usually nice but then you ran away and I didn't like it."

Her lip was quivering but she held his gaze and spoke clearly and honestly. At eight years old she was able to do what he had never been able to until the day before: say to someone that they had hurt her and that she deserved better.

Wes was so ashamed. He was so damned proud of her.

"You're right," he said. "You're right, Gus. I was a bad friend. I got scared, and instead of being honest about it, I ran away. I'm not as brave as you and your dad. I guess I still have a lot to learn about how to be a good friend. About how to be...part of a family."

He ventured this last tentatively, hoping Adam would hear it for the offer it was.

Adam blinked back tears.

Gus was unyielding.

"Family shouldn't run away," she said. "That's what Papa did and Daddy said that he didn't want to be our family."

Adam's eyes widened.

"I didn't say that," he said.

"Yes you did," Gus insisted. "To River."

"Thought you were asleep," Adam muttered.

"Well I don't *want* Papa to be my family anyway." She wrinkled her brow in thought. "And I don't wanna call him Papa anymore, either."

She had Adam's full attention now.

"Well...what do you want to call him, baby?" Adam asked.

Gus scrunched up her face with anger.

"A very bad word!"

"Okay, you have permission, just this once."

Gus' cheeks flushed as she worked up to it.

"Butt!" she ejaculated triumphantly.

It took every ounce of self-control that Wes possessed not to laugh, and he could see the same struggle in Adam's face. Adam clearly managed it by the slimmest of margins, nodding seriously and pulling Gus into a hug.

Their eyes met over Gus' head and neither of them looked away. Then Adam smiled, and Wes smiled back at him.

Chapter Twenty-Seven

Adam

"What do you think?" Adam asked Gus as he kissed her good-night.

Her previous severity had been softened by dinner, winning at Uno, and sleepiness. Now she closed her eyes and smiled softly.

"I love Wes," she said. "I think people deserve a second chance."

Adam's heart felt too large to be contained in any human form.

"Me too, baby," he said. "Me too."

In the living room, Wes had put the crackling fire on TV and lit the tree, bathing everything in a warm glow.

He stood, reticently, until Adam gestured him onto the couch and pulled the blanket over both of them.

"If you're too tired to talk, I understand," Wes said.

Adam was tired, but he'd missed Wes so damn much, and been so damn sad without him, that there was no way he was putting this off for even a minute.

"No, I'm ready."

Adam forced himself to sit quietly as Wes sorted

through his words. He forced himself not to forgive Wes before he'd even spoken.

Adam had heard his whole life that he was a pushover. Too quick to forgive; too easy on people.

But the truth was that Adam had never once regretted forgiving someone. Because forgiveness was about him, and not about them at all. He had forgiven his father for being a bad parent, even though he had no interest in ever seeing him again. He'd forgiven his mother for being a coward. He'd forgiven friends for not coming around anymore after he became a father. Forgiven Marina for not being able to take care of Gus. And Mason...well, okay, he wasn't quite there yet with Mason.

He carried a deep well of forgiveness inside him and when he doled it out it gave him peace and never diminished. It was, he believed, the thing that rescued him from the deep damage of other people's failures. That he had the power to forgive, and in forgiving heal his own wounds without needing the instrument of them anymore.

Wes took a deep breath and Adam knew he could see the promise of forgiveness in his eyes.

"The other night, when I left your house. After all those people came? The newscaster stuck a camera in my face. She thought I was you at first, I guess, but I wasn't thinking clearly. It was like I was right back there, people taking my picture and trying to cut off locks of my hair and writing about what I ate for breakfast. I...I just panicked."

Adam nodded. He was relieved to have called it right.

"I kind of realized that's maybe what happened. Those people coming to take pictures… I didn't even think about your past. I guess, if I'm honest, I didn't understand it was as much of a phobia for you as it is."

"It's… I don't mean to react the way I do. But after that time in my life, I never felt normal. People *were* always staring at me, and I hated it so much, and had such a clear strategy of just kind of freezing and being a nonperson. Being the fake person they were taking a picture of instead of myself, so it wasn't me they were seeing."

Adam remembered the way Wes had frozen at the car outside Gus' school the day of her show-and-tell.

"Even years later, every time someone looked at me, I felt that way. So I started hating *anyone* looking at me. And that led to me not wanting to be in public because that was a sure way to avoid being looked at. So when that lady stuck her camera in my face, all I could think was *Shit, they found me*. And even after I got inside and calmed down cuz I realized it wasn't about me, I still…"

He trailed off and Adam got scared.

"I still knew that if I…if I was with you. Part of a family with you and Gus… I couldn't do that. I couldn't hide in my house. I would have to do things like go to parent-teacher night and go to her science fairs and take you out to dinner."

A look of horror passed over Wes' face.

"Sorry, I don't mean those are bad things. I just mean… I never thought I'd do them. Never. I thought if I was just by myself I could be…"

"Safe," Adam supplied.

"Yeah."

Wes took Adam's hand, and the feel of those gentle, rough hands after days without them nearly brought Adam to tears of relief.

"But I don't *want* to be safe like that. Not if it means missing out on this. On you. You and Gus." Wes' eyes burned. "Have I messed it up too much? Have I lost you?"

"No. But Gus was right. I was pretty heartbroken, Wes. I thought you were just done. I thought you'd thrown us away."

"Like Mason did," Wes murmured.

And there was that. But not exactly.

"Different than Mason. Because Mason didn't know what he was getting, and you did. And you seemed to like what you were getting."

"I did! I do. I really, really do."

Adam smiled.

"The thing is, if we're together, it really *is* about me and Gus. It would be serious pretty fast, because I'm not going to have someone in Gus' life that she could lose this easily."

Wes winced. "When she was telling me off earlier, I was so ashamed. This eight-year-old knows how to ask for what she needs and be honest and I don't. Obviously she gets that from you. So maybe…is it too much to ask that maybe you could help show me?"

It was exactly what Adam wanted to hear. Not empty assurances that Wes would never get scared again, or would be perfect from hereon out. But a request for help in becoming the kind of person that Adam needed, of his own volition.

"I could do that."

Wes leaned in. He stroked Adam's hair and Adam felt electricity dance on his skin.

"I missed you so much," he said.

"I missed you too. I um. I told my dad he was a bad, selfish parent. On his birthday. Whoops."

"You did? Whoa."

"Yeah, and I know that's because of you. Seeing the kind of parent you are to Gus showed me that I wasn't delusional about my dad. So really, you've shown me how to be more honest already. Thank you."

Wes pressed his forehead against Adam's. He smelled like home.

"I'm proud of you," Adam said.

He felt Wes shiver, then the arms he'd missed so dreadfully wrapped around him and pulled him close.

"I love you, Adam," Wes said. "I really love you. And Gus. And I'm so damn sorry I was such a coward."

Adam cupped his face.

"You weren't a coward, baby. You got triggered and had a reaction to something you never fully dealt with. If it happens again, hopefully you'll know that you can tell me."

Wes nodded miserably.

"Hey, Wes?"

"Yeah?"

Adam looked into the beautiful, warm eyes of his brilliant, kind, generous, sweet weirdo.

"I love you too."

Wes blinked, and his expression reminded Adam of Gus' when they'd seen the magical glow of lights this evening.

"Thank you," Wes said. "Thank you, thank you."

He squeezed Adam so tight he almost couldn't breathe, and it was the best breathlessness Adam had ever felt.

Held tight and secure in Wes' arms, Adam felt brave.

"Do you wanna know a secret?" he whispered.

"Always," Wes said immediately.

Adam took a deep breath.

"I think I've loved you almost from the start. And I want to be a family with you. Like, now. I just…"

But he didn't have to explain anything, because Wes was holding him so tight and murmuring words of love into his hair.

Wes lifted him up and carried him like something in a swoony old movie, dropping him on the bed and moving over him, all heat and strength and intense care.

"Wes, I missed you so much."

Wes tipped Adam's head back and kissed him, and Adam could feel every bit of love and desire returned.

"Want everything with you," Wes murmured.

With.

It was exactly what Adam wanted to hear, and he opened his arms, welcoming Wes home.

They held each other, snuggled under the covers, and Adam listened to Wes breathe. Listened to his heartbeat. Smelled his skin and his hair. Every now and then, their mouths would find each other in a kiss.

"I love you," Adam said, pressing a kiss to Wes' chin.

"I love you so much I can't believe it," Wes said.

"You can't believe you love me?" Adam asked.

"I can't believe you exist. I can't believe how wonderful you are. And Gus. Can't believe you want me. Can't believe I'm not still hiding in my house. I can't believe any of it."

Adam didn't try and stop the tears from coming this time. He just shrugged and let Wes kiss them away.

"Merry Christmas," he said.

Then he sat up so fast he almost cracked Wes' skull.

"Oh, no!" Adam said.

"What's wrong?" Wes looked alarmed.

"I don't have a present for you cuz you dumped me."

He was genuinely forlorn. Wes snorted.

"I think the second half of that sentence excuses the first."

"Oh. Right. Asshole," he said, jokingly.

"I'm very sorry," Wes said, not joking at all. "If it makes you feel any better, I don't have a present for you either. Or Gus. Wow, great start to this whole being a family thing, huh?"

All joking aside, Adam lay back down next to Wes. "Having you here for Christmas and every day after is the best gift I can possibly imagine."

Wes stroked his hair and relaxed, pulling the covers over them.

They entwined in the perfect configuration and Adam felt himself start to doze off. He was exhausted.

"Oh, I should warn you," he managed to get out just before sleep took him. "Gus wakes up *very* early on Christmas morning."

He thought maybe Wes said something like *That's okay* or *I love you*, but he wasn't sure because relaxed in the arms of his beloved, sleep came easily.

Chapter Twenty-Eight

Adam

Christmas dawned—well, it didn't quite dawn *anything* because before the sun had risen, Adam was pulled from a deep slumber wrapped in Wes' warm arms by the sound of someone bouncing excitedly outside his door while trying very hard not to make noise.

He nuzzled close to Wes, enjoying his smell for a moment, then, knowing what would happen any second, pressed a kiss to his jaw and whispered, "I'm sorry."

As if attuned to Adam even in sleep, Wes mumbled a sleepy, "Whatswrongbaby?"

Adam stroked his hair, then slid out of bed and into pajamas. He got back into bed and made sure the covers were completely covering Wes' gorgeous body.

"Come in, sweetie," Adam called just as Gus' control broke, and she cried, "Daddy, it's Christmassssss!"

Wes jolted awake as Gus flew through the air and landed in the middle of the bed.

"Get up, get up, it's Christmas!" she crowed, throwing her arms around Adam.

Wes rubbed his eyes as if Adam's apology had just registered, and slid his clothes on under the covers.

"I'm up," Adam assured her. "Go into the living room and turn on the tree and we'll be out in a minute."

"Okay!"

She bounced off the bed and down the hall and strains of a tuneless "It's Christmas, it's Christmas" carol grew fainter as she went.

"Um," Adam said by way of apology.

"Hey. C'mere."

Adam let himself be gathered back into Wes' arms.

"Merry Christmas," Wes said. "I love you."

It was absolutely, positively, without a doubt, the best Christmas present Adam had ever gotten.

"I love you," Adam murmured, kissing him.

They dragged themselves out of bed.

"That's not very cozy," Adam said, indicating the heavy jeans and sweater Wes had pulled on from the night before. "You could go home and get pajamas if you want? Pajama Christmas. It's a thing."

Wes smiled, but hesitated, then shook his head.

"Do you not own pajamas or something?"

"Huh? Oh. Well, I don't, actually, but it's not that."

"What, then?"

"It's silly."

Adam tipped Wes' chin up so he could look into his eyes.

"Say it anyway."

"I'm afraid if I leave I'll realize this was a dream

and I never came here and you never forgave me and everything will be back like it was."

"Oh, baby." Adam pulled him into a hug and stroked his back. "It's not a dream."

"Yeah, well, that's what you'd say if it were a dream too," Wes muttered. Adam couldn't refute that.

"Okay, well, do you want to borrow something of mine instead? It'll be a little small but I have sweats and stuff in there."

"Thanks," Wes said, pulling off the jeans.

"I'll see you downstairs."

"For Christmas," Wes said, like he was still processing it.

Adam didn't mind. He'd give Wes every reassurance he needed because Wes had given the same to him.

"Yup, for Christmas with me and Gus and River."

Adam kissed him and gave his ass a friendly squeeze.

The tree was twinkling and the TV fire was blazing and Gus was sitting suspiciously innocently on the couch.

Adam narrowed his eyes and her gaze cut over to the tree, but she just smiled.

"How about pancakes?" he asked, and she nodded.

While he was pouring the first one onto the griddle, Wes came downstairs wearing Adam's clothes.

Adam hadn't previously known that it was possible for someone to look simultaneously hot, adorable, and ridiculous, but it turned out that it was. Wes had chosen some blue pajama pants with gold stars on them and an old, paint-spattered yellow sweatshirt that Adam had bought from a fundraiser at Gus' preschool. It said *Proud Parent of Little Tyke* on it in red.

The pajama pants fit Wes almost like leggings. They were clearly too short, so he'd borrowed some of Adam's wool socks and pulled them up to his calves. The sweatshirt was tight on him and too short in the arms. The whole effect was of a child that had chosen their own outfit.

Only, you know. Hot. Because Wes.

Adam didn't mention the outfit because he didn't want to make Wes uncomfortable—especially knowing his feelings about being looked at. Gus had no such compunction.

"You look so funny!" she said. "Those are Daddy's clothes."

"Pajama Christmas. I was told it's a thing," Wes said.

Gus high-fived him.

They ate pancakes and Adam made a double-strong pot of coffee, knowing they'd need their energy. They played several more rounds of Uno with Christmas movies in the background, and Gus had Wes take her around the outside of the house to show her all the lights he'd added to the house, bioluminescent and otherwise.

After that Wes ran home briefly to feed the animals and, he said, get presents. Adam gave him a funny look because Wes had said he didn't have presents, but he returned with several boxes that he instructed them not to touch.

By the time River arrived at 11:30, Gus had consumed too much sugar and taken to running around the living room pretending to be a lyrebird that they'd just learned about from a David Attenborough special.

"Yay, River!" she shouted when they came in the door. "It's Christmas!"

"It is," River said, catching her in a one-armed hug. The other arm was occupied with several boxes.

"Come in," Adam said, winking at them. "Want me to hold that for a minute?"

River put the medium-sized box down gently on the floor to take their boots and coat off.

"It's okay, actually," they said very quietly. "But I think we should do presents sooner rather than later."

"Got it."

Adam left River to get cozy in the living room, and corralled Gus out of the kitchen, where she was trying to add mini candy canes to the Christmas monster cookies they'd made after breakfast, and into the living room.

"Is it presents, is it presents?"

She was bouncing in place. Adam nodded, wiping icing off her eyebrow with his thumb.

"Yay!"

She rocketed through the living room, and upstairs, then back down, with her arms full of three presents wrapped in grocery bags and covered with marker and stickers.

Adam's heart lurched.

"Can I give mine first?" Gus asked.

Adam looked to River who peeked at their box, then nodded.

"Sure, sweetie."

"Okay this is for you, Daddy." She handed him the largest package. "This is for you." She gave a slightly smaller one to River. "And this is yours," she told Wes. "I was working on it before you went away, so now you're back and you get a present."

She smiled when she said it so Adam knew she was just being honest, not trying to make Wes feel bad. From Wes' smile, he knew it too.

Adam opened his first.

It was... He had no idea what it was. There were washers and twists of wire and what appeared to be part of a chrome hubcap. The entire thing was beautiful in a brutal, abstract way.

"Thank you, Gus, it's beautiful," Adam said, hoping that would satisfy her. "Maybe you can show me where I should put it to best appreciate it."

Adam caught Wes' eye and saw the humor there.

"It's an invention!" Gus said. "Can't you tell?"

"I absolutely can," Adam said. Because yes, he taught his daughter not to lie. But there was room for a little fib in some instances.

River and Wes unwrapped their gifts, revealing similarly constructed objects.

"What a cool invention," River told Gus, and Gus beamed.

Wes examined his from every angle, then pronounced it perfect.

Gus looked ecstatic.

"Okay, now me," she said.

Adam nudged the box that River had brought toward her.

"Merry Christmas, sweetheart."

Gus bent down and lifted the lid off the box. Adam held his breath. Then a small orange head popped out.

"I thought, since you wanted a pet so much, we could adopt her," Adam said.

River added, "Her name is Neon, but you can totally change it."

Gus patted the cat's head in the box.

"It's really cute," she said. "Thanks."

Gus' reception of River's gift of a litter box, cat food, and some cat toys was similarly lukewarm. Neon's enthusiasm for the toys in particular was far greater.

Adam's heart sank. Gus had so clearly wanted a pet, he'd thought this would be the perfect gift. He'd wanted so badly to make her happy.

"Um," Wes said, looking conflicted. "At the risk of overcrowding the house…"

He pushed the box he'd brought from his house toward Gus. She lifted the lid just as she had on Adam's gift. But this time, her eyes got wide and her mouth fell open as she gasped with joy. Exactly the response Adam had been hoping for and didn't get.

Suddenly, Adam got a very bad, creepy feeling. His eyes flew to Wes.

"I swear, it's not a tarantula," Wes said immediately.

Adam could breathe again.

Wes reached into the box and extracted…an orange and brown lizard.

"Oh my god, I love him!" Gus cried, stroking the lizard and cuddling it to her chest.

She turned to Adam with big, pleading eyes.

"Can I keep him?"

Over her head, Wes grimaced the grimace of the non-child-having when they realized too late that they should have checked with a parent before giving something to a kid. Luckily for everyone, Adam was fine with it.

"As long as you promise to take very good care of it and as long as I never have to touch it."

"I will!"

Adam turned to River.

"I guess I have a cat now," he said.

River grinned. "You'll love Neon. She's the best."

Truth be told, Adam was delighted to have Neon. And if Gus was happy because of Wes' present and not his? It didn't matter. The only thing that mattered was that she *was* happy.

Adam and River made hot chocolate while Gus and Wes got the lizard (whose name, it turned out, was Ludwig) settled in her bedroom. He'd brought an aquarium for it and a jar that he hid behind his back and told Adam he didn't want to know when Adam asked what was in it.

"So," River said. "You and Wes are okay now?"

Adam nodded.

"He just got scared. But everyone deserves a second chance."

"I'm so happy for you," they said. "And for Gus. She really loves him."

"I know. The feeling's mutual."

Adam imagined Wes helping Gus with her science projects and tramping through the woods with her looking for mushrooms or spiders or whatever the hell people looked for in the woods.

"He's gonna make a really, really good dad," Adam said.

River's eyes got wide, but they nodded.

"I think so too."

"What about you, sweetie? Are you seeing anyone?" Adam asked.

A dreamy, mysterious look passed over River's face.

"Not quite…maybe…there's kind of someone," they said. They were flushing at the thought.

"I'm glad," Adam said, handing them a mug of cocoa.

River left around four, citing the need to get back and give the cats their dinner, but now that Adam knew they were not quite, maybe, kind of seeing someone, he wondered if River didn't have a second stop to make.

Gus, high on Christmas adrenaline, her new lizard, and a day full of sugar and running around, crashed out hard right after dinner. Adam carried her to bed and tucked her in, all without looking at what was in the jar that now sat next to the newly ensconced lizard aquarium.

"Hi, Ludwig," Adam said as he passed the tank, in the spirit of Christmas.

Back in the living room, Wes had collapsed on the sofa, head lolling languidly against the cushion.

Adam arranged himself within Wes' arms and pressed a kiss to his lips.

"So this is Christmas," Wes said.

"Yeah. What do you think?"

"I give it a solid nine," Wes said. "Bumped up to a ten for the part where you got yourself a cat for Christmas."

"Oh my god, I know, but she's so cute."

As if Neon could hear the praise being heaped upon her, she padded into the room, walked in a circle, then plopped down in the exact middle of the living room floor and proceeded to fall instantly and adorably asleep.

"Is it okay to go outside for a minute?" Wes asked. "I wanna show you something."

Adam was pretty sure Gus was down for the count. So he bundled up and followed Wes outside into the front yard.

Wes took a pair of binoculars from his coat pocket. He stood behind Adam and wrapped his arms around him, putting the binoculars up to Adam's eyes.

Adam looked and saw the moon, nearly full, hanging heavy in the velvet sky. Lines crisscrossed the cratered surface. It looked unreal.

"Wow," Adam said.

"Sometimes I go outside at night," Wes said. "I have a telescope I take to the roof. I look at the stars and the moon. It's the most beautiful, expansive, peaceful thing. Vast and quiet. And... I wonder what it would be like if there was someone up there with me."

Wes' arms tightened around Adam's stomach and he rested his chin on Adam's shoulder.

"I'm sorry I don't have a real gift for you. But I thought you might like this."

Adam swallowed around the lump in his throat. He felt a happiness that seemed so large it could launch itself outside his body and find a home glowing brightest among the stars.

"It's so damn beautiful," Adam said, voice thick. "I don't care about presents. I have everything I want."

Adam and Wes stood, huddled together, in front of a house dripping with lights that had come from as far away as New York and as near as across the street. They stood in front of that house that yelled *I love you!* and watched the stars move over Garnet Run, Wyoming, as Christmas settled into a memory in the houses nearby.

Once, the residents of Knockbridge Lane had told stories of Westley Mobray the vampire, the witch, the Satanist, the freak.

But Adam knew better.

Wes Mobray was a brilliant, kind, generous, sexy, romantic weirdo. And he was going to be a part of Adam and Gus' family.

Adam leaned his head back and claimed a kiss from the lips of the most amazing man he'd ever known.

By next year, the residents of Knockbridge Lane would tell a very different story. The love story of Wes Mobray and Adam Mills.

* * * * *

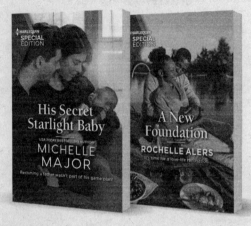

SPECIAL EXCERPT FROM

H HARLEQUIN

SPECIAL EDITION

*Nothing will change how much Colt Dawson loves his
baby boy. Not even the shocking news his deceased wife
lied about Ryder's paternity. But confronting
Ava Guthrie about his ex's sperm-donor scheme doesn't
go as planned. Will Ava heal Colt's betrayed heart in
time for a Wyoming family Christmas?*

Read on for a sneak peek at
His Baby No Matter What,
*the next book in the Dawson Family Ranch miniseries
by Melissa Senate!*

"I wasn't planning on getting one," Ava said. "I figured
it would be make me feel sad, celebrating all alone out at
the ranch. My parents gone too young. And this year, my
great-aunt gone before I even knew her. My best friend
after the worst argument I've ever had. I love Christmas,
but this is a weird one."

"Yeah, it is. And you're not alone. I'm here. Ryder's
here. And like you said, you love Christmas. That house
needs some serious cheering up. I want to get you a tree
as a gift from me to you for our good deal."

"It *is* a good deal," she said. "Okay. A tree. I have a
box of ornaments that I brought over in the move to the
ranch."

He pulled out his phone, did some googling and found a Christmas-tree farm that also sold wreaths just ten minutes from here. He held up the site. "Let's go after Ryder's nap. While he's asleep, we can have that meeting—I mean, *talk*—about our arrangement. Set the agenda. The… What would you call it in noncorporate speak?"

She laughed. "Maybe it is a little nice having a CEO around here," she said, then took a bite of her sandwich. "You get things done, Colt Dawson."

He reached over and touched her hand and she squeezed it. Again he was struck by how close he felt to her. But he had to remember he was leaving in two and a half weeks, going back to Bear Ridge, back to his life. There was a 5 percent chance, probably less, that he'd ever leave Godfrey and Dawson. But he'd have this break, this Christmas with his son, on this alpaca ranch.

With a woman who made him think of reaching for the stars, even if he wouldn't.

Don't miss
His Baby No Matter What *by Melissa Senate,*
available November 2021 wherever
Harlequin Special Edition books and ebooks are sold.

Harlequin.com